The Wistful Scent

of

Lilac

Bobbi Miles

enjoy!

Bobbi Miles

The Wistful Scent of Lilac

ISBN: 9781693366321

Dedicated to Skip, who encouraged me to start this story,

and to Mike, who encouraged me to finish it.

To Joshua and Rebecca: We are still a family.

Nothing is more wistful than the scent of lilac,

nor more robust than its woody stalk,

for we must remember that it is a tree as well as a flower,

we must try not to forget this.

—*Stevie Smith*

CHAPTER 1

The air was cool on that Sunday morning in early autumn. Eldri and her friend, Anna, were busy in the muggy kitchen at Brotvik's Boardinghouse, and they were glad for the light breeze coming through the open windows. Eldri had just pulled the last piece of fried chicken out of the hot skillet. After shaking off the excess oil, she set it on the toweled plate with the rest of the pieces. While waiting for the chicken and the remains of the oil in the skillet to cool, she took the freshly baked bread out of the oven. From a shelf in the pantry, Anna pulled two jars of the pickles she'd canned in the summer. Then she poured fresh tea into two glass bottles and plugged them tightly.

Next, they wrapped a few hard-boiled eggs into bright red and white checkered napkins and put the red potatoes they had boiled a little earlier into two small bowls. They gathered the plates, silverware, and cups they would need, along with a few more of the cheerful napkins, and put them into the bottom of two large baskets. When the bread had cooled a bit, Anna put one loaf in her basket and the other into Eldri's. Next, she gingerly divided the warm chicken pieces, then wrapped and tied the portions in butcher paper to absorb any remaining oil, all the while trying not to burn her fingers. Only after everything else was packed did Eldri set the fresh cherry pie into Anna's basket and the rich chocolate cake into her own.

"Anna, do you think anyone will bid on my picnic basket?"

"No one will be able to resist our fried chicken or your chocolate cake, Eldri."

"I hope you are right. You are lucky to know that Alf is going to win your basket."

"He'd better."

"Of course, he will. And, I sure do hope that whoever wins mine will be someone as nice as Alf, since I will have to spend all afternoon with him." To herself, Eldri added, maybe that Ole Larsen will bid on my basket. I think I would not mind spending an afternoon with him.

Once the food was packed and ready to go, the young women hung their aprons on a hook in the kitchen.

"Come on, we need to hurry," Eldri called down to her friend as she started up to the room she and Anna shared to finish getting ready for the day, full basket in hand in case any of Mrs. Brotvik's boarders were tempted to sneak into the kitchen and sample its contents.

"I'm hurrying, I'm hurrying."

"Did you bring your basket?" Eldri asked.

"Ya, ya. But it's awfully heavy to be dragging up these

stairs," Anna grumbled.

After retucking her starched white shirtwaist into her dark navy skirt, buckling her black silk belt, buttoning the tops of her black leather boots and, with a distracted swipe, tucking an errant lock of brown hair behind her right ear, Eldri opened the small closet door, took her cotton coat off the hanger, then pulled her straw boater from the shelf above. Eldri would not wear her good hat—the oversized, mushroom-shaped, black felt with red roses and a wide, red satin band—to church today. Because of the picnic afterward, she didn't want to risk damaging it—there wasn't the money for a new one.

"Anna, are you wearing your boater today, too? And your coat? I can get them for you."

"Don't bother, Eldri, I'll get them."

Eldri wasn't very tall, but she could at least reach the top shelf of the closet by standing on her toes. There was no hope, though, for Anna. "You cannot reach the shelf without stepping onto that old chair in the corner. And we both know, if you do, you will put your foot right through its seat. So, tell me, the boater or your regular church hat?"

"I suppose you're right. The boater, please."

After Anna finished pinning up her hair, she took her hat and coat from Eldri. Anna's fiancé, Alf, had already knocked on the front door and was waiting for her on the porch of the boardinghouse, so she hurriedly slipped on her coat and hat and grabbed her basket.

"Bye, Eldri. I'll save you a seat," Anna shouted as she dashed down the stairs to meet Alf and walk to church.

Eldri picked up her own basket and came downstairs a few minutes later, much quieter than her friend had done, and, resting her hand on the doorknob, announced, "I am leaving now, Mrs. Brotvik."

"Uff da. That Anna. Always makes such a big racket, stomping down my stairs and slamming the front door. And then there's you, sneaking out so quietly like you're hiding something. Did you clean up after yourselves? And did you leave enough food for the folks here? Since you were in my kitchen all morning, you know *I* couldn't do any cooking."

Eldri sighed. "Ya, ya, Mrs. Brotvik, we are finished with your kitchen, and it is clean. Anna and I appreciate that you let us use it this morning. And there is plenty of chicken, potatoes, and bread for everyone."

"And there is dessert?"

"Ya, there are two cherry pies cooling in the window. If you have nothing else, it is nearly time for church, and I should be leaving."

"Always in a hurry. Go on, then."

Walking out the front door, Eldri looked up at the gray sky and hoped it wouldn't rain. "Please, not today," she whispered to no one in particular. But then, resigned to the fact she had no control over the weather, Eldri breathed in the crisp morning air, checked that her basket was well-covered, and began the short walk to church.

Eldri enjoyed the community of Conway's Norwegian Lutheran Church, but she had to admit she also looked forward to the respite it provided from Mrs. Brotvik's suffocating presence. Both Eldri and Anna knew that if Mrs. Brotvik had her way, she would have them working seven days a week. Even Mrs. Brotvik couldn't argue with God, though, and she gave the girls the Lord's Day off—grudgingly. Eldri thought it a shame Mrs. Brotvik didn't go to church herself. Perhaps it would soften her sharp edges. But Eldri couldn't argue with Mrs. Brotvik any more successfully than Mrs. Brotvik could argue with God. Pitiful as Mrs. Brotvik's life was, Eldri knew of nothing she could do to help the woman.

Those troublesome thoughts preoccupied Eldri from the moment she left the boardinghouse until she arrived at the pair of heavy fir doors that guarded the small, white clapboard church.

"Ah, well, nothing to be done about Mrs. Brotvik or the weather, at least for now, and I will not let them ruin the rest of my Sunday," Eldri mumbled as she opened one of the doors.

She soon found her friends and sat down next to Anna in the hard-seat, stiff-backed wooden pew. "No chance to be lulled asleep in this church, however dull the sermon," she whispered to Anna while she tried, unsuccessfully, to make herself comfortable.

"Hush, Eldri." Anna giggled a little too loudly and paid for it with the glare of several pairs of stern-eyed parishioners. She hung her head down a little, in mock penance, but the grin remained on her face.

Ole Larsen came in a few minutes later, took off his hat, nodded a greeting to Anna and Eldri, and sat down on the other side of Alf. Eldri nodded back, then felt her cheeks get warm.

Alf had laughed when his friend started showing up in church a few months ago. "I see you've found religion, Ole," he'd teased.

"Oh, ya, it's religion I've found." Ole had said, smiling, as he'd glanced over Eldri's way.

The service was conducted in Norwegian, of course. Most of the folks in that rural Skagit Valley community had their roots in Norway and, like Eldri, many hadn't learned much English. On that Sunday, however, it didn't matter if the sermon was in English or Norwegian, or even whether it was dull or riveting. All the worshippers were hoping for was brevity because the sooner the service ended, the sooner the picnic basket auction could begin.

Not long into his sermon, the Reverend Torgersen noticed the fidgeting and heard the stomach rumblings of his impatient congregants, and he kept his message mercifully short. Of course, he might have been just as eager for the picnic as everyone else. He'd spent the early morning trying to concentrate on his sermon notes without becoming distracted by the mouth-watering smells that wafted from the parsonage kitchen while his wife prepared their own picnic lunch.

Naturally, Alf made sure he placed the winning bid for his girl's basket. And the other men who were also one-half of a couple were wise enough to follow suit. The exciting part of the auction came when it was time for the single men in the congregation to bid on the baskets that had been prepared by the single women. Eldri was excited for the bidding to start on the lunch she and Anna had so carefully prepared—until, that is, the widowed farmer from down the road, who Eldri felt certain never went near a bathtub, shouted out the first bid. Fortunately, Ole soon looked over at her and winked. Then he, too, joined the competition.

When the bidding ended, Anna clapped her hands. "Ole won your basket!" Relieved and secretly pleased, Eldri gave her friend a shy smile while the farmer, sore loser that he was, harrumphed and glared at Ole. Then, stuffing his hands deep into his overall pockets, he stomped out of the church.

Chuckling over the display of poor sportsmanship, Ole and Alf collected their winnings, then walked over to the church's entryway, where Eldri and Anna were waiting, Alf asked, "Ladies, what do you say to the four of us eating together down by the river?"

"Perfect," replied Anna.

"And you, Eldri? Think you can stand to have lunch with these two?" Ole nodded toward Anna and Alf.

"Ya, maybe." Eldri smiled.

"Hey, wait. Alf, I think we've just been insulted. Don't you?" asked Anna.

"No, but only because I'm too hungry to look for new friends to eat with. Come on, Anna, and you two, let's find a good spot to eat."

Alf offered his free arm to Anna. Modeling his friend, Ole extended—actually, thrust more than extended—an arm in Eldri's direction. Eldri smiled at the attempted courtesy, however clumsy, and looped her right arm into Ole's left.

"Uh, do you like dogs, Eldri?"

"I do not know where that question came from, but, yes, I suppose so. Why?"

"Well, I have this dog. Her name is Gus, and I'm sure she would love to join us."

"That is okay to me, but only if you tell me why a girl dog is named Gus." Looking around, Eldri saw no sign of a dog. "And, where is she?"

Ole let out a whistle and up popped a head over the side of his wagon. In what seemed a single, swift motion, Gus looked in the direction of the whistle, leapt out of the wagon, and bounded over to Ole's side, but not before knocking Eldri sideways a little.

"Uff da, Ole, you do have a faithful friend here," Eldri said as she reached down to scratch Gus's head and scruff her neck.

"Careful, Eldri, what you're doing there is about all it will take for Gus to become your faithful friend, too." Ole smiled.

The ominous gray clouds of the early morning had given way to a beautiful blue afternoon sky filled with fat, white cotton ball clouds. The two couples walked the short distance from the church to the bank of the Skagit River and found a spot, shaded by the leaves of a wild lilac tree, under which to spread the cotton blanket Ole had grabbed from the wagon. Anna and Eldri set out the contents of their baskets while Alf and Ole waited, as patiently as their hungry stomachs would allow, for the feast that filled the air with a mouth-watering combination of smells—fried chicken, still-warm bread, cherry pie, and chocolate cake.

"Now, tell me, how did you come to have a dog named Gus?" Eldri asked.

Reluctantly, Ole delayed his first bite of the tempting fried chicken in order to tell Gus's story.

"Feel free to chime in, Alf." Ole looked over Alf who, mouth too full to speak, simply held up his right hand and waved his refusal with a half-eaten drumstick.

"You're no help. Well, anyway, one night last August, Alf and I, and the rest of the men at the logging camp, were relaxing around an outside fire. There wasn't much in the way of conversation. We'd had a long, hard day up on the hillside. Then this one showed up." Ole nodded toward Gus. "She wandered through our crowd and sniffed around at the campfire smoke, burning tobacco, and the smelly men."

Clearing his throat with a choked laugh, Alf defended himself. "Hey Ole, watch who you're calling smelly."

"Ya, ya, after the day we'd had, you know you were one of them. So was I," Ole replied. "Anyway, this girl here, she looked around, then decided to set herself down next to me. The men laughed that I'd gotten myself a new girlfriend, but she ignored them. So did I. The next sound we all heard was her snoring. And, boy oh boy, did she snore. There was no telling how far she'd wandered, but one thing was sure, it had worn her out.

"Tired as she was, though, when I got up to get her some scraps from the cook's tent, she got up, too. And when I settled into my bunk for the night, she settled herself down next to it. I figured if I was who she was looking for, then it was okay by me. She's good-natured and easy to have around."

"And the name? Gus?" asked Eldri.

"It's pretty simple. She showed up at the camp in August, it's the same word in Norwegian and English, you know, so I decided to name her Augusta. Gus for short. When I asked her what she thought of her new name, her ears perked up and she nudged my hand, which was hanging over the side of my bunk. I took that to mean she was okay with it. So, Gus it is," Ole said as he finally bit into the piece of chicken he'd forgone eating in favor of telling Gus's story.

All that time, Gus had been sunning herself on a warm rock nearby, but when she heard her name, she lumbered back over to the picnickers. This time, she sat down next to Eldri and nudged her hand.

"I like that story, Ole." Eldri scratched Gus's head absent-mindedly. "How old do you think she is? What kind of dog is she?"

"Well, she's not a puppy, but still pretty young—three or four, maybe—and her coloring is shepherd. But mostly she's just a mutt."

"A rather nice mutt, I would say." Eldri leaned down toward Gus's face. "I think you made a good choice when you picked that man."

This time, it was Ole whose face warmed and cheeks reddened.

"Oh, boy, all this sweet talk is too much for me," Alf teased. "Come on, Anna, let's take a walk. I need to digest some of the food you overfed me."

"The only person who overfed you is you!" Anna laughed.

"Wait a minute, though. Before we go, why don't you take a photo of Eldri and Ole?"

Alf grabbed his new Kodak Brownie camera and stood. When Eldri and Ole were ready, he looked down, into the viewfinder of the black, leatherette box. "Smile, you two. Well, three, if you count Gus."

"Now, let me take a photo of you and Anna," said Ole. Alf handed the camera over.

"How does it work?" asked Eldri.

"I'll show you. Come over here and look into that small, round window on top." Eldri moved in closer to Ole, and he pointed to the viewfinder.

"Do you see Alf and Anna in there?"

"I do!"

"Good, then hold the camera very still and push down on the shutter lever."

Eldri did as instructed and looked up at Ole. "What do I do next?"

"That's all there is to it. You're officially a photographer now."

After the photo shoot and lesson were over, Ole watched Alf and Anna walk away, hand in hand. "Everyone should be so lucky to find each other as they have been," he said.

"Yes."

"Can I ask you ... I hope you don't mind ... well, do you think much about marriage?"

"I do not mind and, ya, sure I do. What girl my age does not?" Eldri laughed.

"That's funny?"

"Nei, Ole, I am sorry. It is not your question that is funny. I was thinking about my sister, Marta. I do not think she will ever marry."

"Why is that?"

"She is just so independent and doesn't want to rely on anyone but herself."

"But you, Eldri, do you feel that way, too?"

"Ole, I can think of nothing better than living the rest of my life with a good man in a home of my own that is filled with lots of noisy children." Eldri covered her mouth with her hand. "Forgive me. I am not usually so forward."

"Not forward, Eldri. Just honest. And when a person is simply being honest, there is nothing to forgive. Besides, I can see you living that life, and I would be happy for you. Hopefully, there is a good man somewhere near."

"Thank you, Ole, perhaps there is." Looking up at the tree that had shaded them all afternoon, Eldri said, "Lilacs. They are my favorite."

"The flowers seem so delicate, but the tree itself is actually quite strong. I think maybe that's how you are, too."

"Uhm, well, I don't know. Anyway, we should get these things packed up and find Alf and Anna," Eldri said.

"Ya, it's probably time," Ole said as the two of them

placed the few remains of their lunch into the basket, their hands lightly touching.

"I hope your lunch was worth the price you paid."

"The lunch was worth more, much more, than every penny I paid," Ole replied. "Come on, Gus."

After finding Alf and Anna near the church, the young people loaded their things into Ole's wagon. Alf lifted Anna into the back, then climbed in next to her, nearly tangling up with an eager and excited Gus. Ole helped Eldri into the seat at the front of the wagon, hiked himself up, and took the reins.

Except for the rhythmic clatter of the turning wagon wheels and the regular whine of a snoring Gus, the ride back to Conway was quiet until Ole pulled up the wagon next to the worn plank sidewalk below Mrs. Brotvik's front steps. Alf was the first out, jumping down so he could help Anna. But Eldri and Ole lingered a moment.

"Thank you, Ole. This was perhaps the best day I have had since coming to Conway."

"Me, too, Eldri."

"You? But you have been here so much longer than I have. You must have had better days than this one."

"No, Eldri, I have not. This was surely my best day," Ole said as he climbed down then put his hands around Eldri's slim waist to lift her down.

Alf and Anna were already at the front door, where

Anna gave Alf a hug and kiss on the cheek. And then the two young women reluctantly went inside. Tomorrow was going to be a busy day—Mondays at Mrs. Brotvik's always were—but, tired though they were, Eldri and Anna still needed to clean up the remains of the picnic before going to their room.

CHAPTER 2

"He likes you." Anna winked at her friend.

"Hush, now. It was a simple lunch together."

"The way the two of you were looking at each other, I think it was more than a *simple* lunch."

"You do get ahead of yourself sometimes, Anna. But I will tell you this was a wonderful day, and spending the afternoon with Mr. Larsen was the best part of it."

"Mmm-hmm," Anna muttered.

"Oh, stop. Come on, now, let us get these things cleaned up. It has been a long day, and the morning will be here much too soon."

The young women finished washing the dishes and putting them away. They piled up the napkins for Monday's wash and set the baskets back on the pantry shelf. When they finally started up the stairs, Mrs. Brotvik bellowed from the front room of the boardinghouse. "I hope you left the kitchen as you found it. Nice enough of me to loan you my things for a silly picnic, but I won't be cleaning up after you."

"All is as we found it, Mrs. Brotvik. Thank you," replied Eldri.

No response.

"Good night, Mrs. Brotvik." Anna said, sticking out her tongue.

"Anna!" Eldri whispered at her friend, held her hand to her mouth, and tried, unsuccessfully, to stifle a giggle.

"What's that you say?" asked Mrs. Brotvik.

"Nothing," Eldri said, choking through her giggle.

"Watch your tone, young lady," came in response.

"I will try, Mrs. Brotvik. Good night," sighed Eldri.

Anna rolled her eyes, Eldri shook her head, and they continued up the stairs.

While Eldri and Anna were cleaning up in Mrs. Brotvik's kitchen, Ole and Alf headed back to the logging camp.

"A good day, wouldn't you say, Ole?"

"A very good day."

"I think Eldri likes you."

"Do you? Because I surely do like her. Yup, I like her very much, and I look forward to seeing her again."

"When we all go to the courthouse next Friday, maybe you can make that another good day."

"Maybe I can, Alf, maybe I can."

When Friday came around, it held such promise. As usual, Eldri was the first one awake. She got out of the bed she had shared with Anna for the last year and wiped the damp off the little window of the room. The rising sun was starting to gleam over the morning dew. The deep green leaves on the trees, the green that comes just before a leaf turns color and falls off, and the petals on the last of the September flowers seemed decorated with tiny crystals. And then there was the chill of an early autumn morning that often portended a cold winter.

Eldri shivered and wrapped her shawl tightly around her narrow shoulders, turned away from the window, and smiled at her lazy friend. "Wake up, Anna. It looks like a beautiful day for a wedding."

"Just a minute more, please, Eldri. It's so warm in this bed and so cold out there."

"No, Anna. Up you go." Eldri threw the coverlet back.

"Cruel girl."

"Not cruel, Anna, just anxious to get done with our chores so we can go get you married."

Sighing dramatically, and loudly enough to be certain Eldri would hear, Anna reluctantly climbed out of the cozy bed.

Ignoring her friend's theatrics, Eldri slipped out of her nightgown and into her housedress. She had filled the chipped ceramic pitcher from the pump outside the night before so she and Anna would have fresh water in the morning, something she did every evening. Anna shrieked as she splashed that water, fresh but oh so cold, on her cheeks. Facing the mirror and pinning up her long, brown hair, Eldri looked past her own reflection and smiled in the direction of her friend.

It hadn't been easy getting the afternoon off. Mrs. Brotvik wasn't generous with favors, especially so soon after lending out her kitchen. When Eldri had assured Mrs. Brotvik that she and Anna would get all their chores done before leaving early, Mrs. Brotvik's only response was to ask, "If you can get your chores done in part of a day, why do I pay you for a whole day?" Mrs. Brotvik's sister in Brooklyn, Eldri's Tante Lena, was as sweet as Mrs. Brotvik was bitter, and Eldri could only imagine her aunt's sadness were she to know that her sister had turned so sour.

The young women went down the stairs and into the kitchen and poured their morning coffee. It wasn't very good, but it was hot. The oatmeal mush Mrs. Brotvik had made earlier and left on the stove was much the same.

"I'm not going to miss it here. And I'm especially not going to miss Mrs. Brotvik. But you, Eldri? I am surely going to miss you."

Eldri shushed Anna, good-naturedly, of course, then gave her a hug. "Come on. Time for us to get to work. We have a lot to do before Alf and Ole get here." Eldri knew Anna could have taken the morning off. After all, it was her wedding day, so she wouldn't be returning to Mrs. Brotvik's at day's end. But without Anna's help, Eldri would never finish all there was to do in time to go with her friend to the courthouse in Mount Vernon. Eldri also wondered how, without Anna, she was going to get everything done tomorrow, and the next day, and the next. She knew Mrs. Brotvik wouldn't hire a new girl even one day earlier than she had to, but she did hope Mrs. Brotvik would do it soon.

"You're right, Eldri. I guess we might as well start by clearing the breakfast dishes from the dining room."

"Ya. Dishes first, then we can make up the beds. I am glad we do not have to wash sheets today."

By late morning, Eldri and Anna had finished the chores: Dishes were washed and put away, beds were made, floors were swept, and the parlor was dusted. They had also managed to ignore Mrs. Brotvik with her stony face and her stiff back, arms crossed over her ample bosom. Sorry as Eldri might have felt for Mrs. Brotvik and her misery, wherever it came from, she would not allow it to dampen the mood of Alf's and Anna's wedding day any more than she had allowed it to affect last Sunday's lovely picnic.

At the same time that Eldri was braiding and pinning up Anna's fine hair, Alf was helping Ole hitch up the sturdy horses to the wagon. They also secured the second seat and attached the canopy. It was not a work wagon today.

Alf and Ole had arranged to be at the boardinghouse at noon, and they pulled the horses and wagon in front precisely on time.

"What's up with you, Alf? All the way here, you've been still and quiet as the dead, and now you start shaking?" Ole asked.

"I don't know what's up with me except all of a sudden, I have no idea what I'm doing."

"You're about to take what will probably be the biggest step of your life. You've also had plenty of time to think about it and figure out if you're sure you want to do this. Now it's time to be a man. Go get Anna. And, stop shaking, dammit, or, I swear, you're gonna make this wagon fall apart before we even start for Mount Vernon."

"Christ, Ole. I'm going, I'm going." Alf tenuously hopped down, walked up to the front door, and knocked.

"Wait here," was all Mrs. Brotvik said before closing the door and leaving Alf pacing on the porch. Ole was just as glad to be outside, where it was bright and sunny, and certainly more pleasant, than inside Brotvik's. Ole was glad for the good weather, too, because riding in the wagon over rutted, dry roads to get to the courthouse was far more comfortable than riding in sloppy rain over rutted, muddy ones.

While he waited, Ole's thoughts turned to Alf and Anna. He knew some folks in Conway thought them an unlikely couple. Alf was as tall and lean as his name, while Anna was short and wide as her own. To see them on the street, folks might think them an awkward pair, but they would not be more wrong. Alf and Anna completed each other. Ole laughed to himself at the thought that Anna was especially good at completing Alf's sentences.

The front door opened, and Alf's eyes got big. "Anna. You look ..."

"Beautiful?" asked Anna.

"You do. You look beautiful." Alf struggled to maintain what little composure he'd managed to gather while waiting at the door. "So, you sure you want to do this?"

"I guess we might as well, because neither of us seems to be finding anyone else we'd rather be with," Anna teased as she took Alf's arm. "You coming, Eldri?"

"I am right behind you." Eldri looked toward the wagon, then over at Ole. "No Gus today?"

"I take Gus nearly everywhere I go. But weddings? Nope, not weddings," he replied.

Eldri smiled and let Ole help her into the wagon.

On the way to Mount Vernon, Ole kept thinking about the idea he'd had after last Sunday's picnic and wondering if it was really as good as he thought. But, by the time he pulled the wagon in front of the courthouse, he'd convinced himself it was, in fact, a *very* good idea. So, when Ole had the chance, he pulled Alf aside and let him know what he was planning.

Alf replied, "Are you sure about this, Ole?"

"I am. I've been thinking about it for a while, and, after the church picnic, I was convinced."

"Well, okay, then."

The judge entered the courtroom. "Good afternoon, folks. Are we ready?"

"We are," exclaimed Anna.

"May I have a moment, your honor?" Ole asked the judge.

While Ole was talking to the judge, in a hushed tone, Eldri noticed the two of them looking in her direction and smiling. Curious, she thought. But soon enough, Ole and the judge had rejoined the group, and Eldri let go of her curiosity.

"Shall we get started on these papers? First of all, I need some signatures. Here and here, here and here," said the judge, pointing at blank lines on the various documents. Eldri was visibly relieved to have Ole's help in showing her where to sign her name.

When all the paperwork was in order, the judge directed Alf and Anna to face him on his right side, Ole and Eldri to face him on his left. Eldri smiled and moved over next to Ole and, on his cue, said yes to both questions asked of her by the judge.

The ceremony took only a few minutes, and after

shaking everyone's hands, the judge escorted the two couples out of the building. "My congratulations to you all," he said with a smile and a wave after locking the courthouse doors and starting for home.

"Oh Eldri, I'm so happy for us."

"Ya, Anna, I am very happy for you and Alf."

"But not just for Alf and me. For you and Ole, too."

"What are you talking about, Anna?"

"Silly goose, I'm talking about you marrying Ole."

"I what?"

"You and Ole. You just married Ole."

"I sure did not. I think I would know if I had gotten married."

"Oh, oh. This is not good." Anna glared at Alf.

Eldri didn't hear Anna's last comment. She was too busy marching down the courthouse steps and over to Ole, who was busy checking on his horses.

"Ole Larsen!"

Ole turned around, and with a big smile on his face, replied, "Eldri?"

"Please tell Anna that she has misunderstood the ceremony. She thinks we got married, too. Tell her she is mistaken."

"There's no mistake, Eldri. We did just get married. You're Eldri Larsen now. A nice name, don't you think?"

"I am who? No, no, and no. I am Eldri Holm."

"No longer, Eldri. When the judge married Alf and Anna, he married us, too, and your new name is Eldri Larsen. Here's our marriage certificate." Ole showed Eldri the official-looking paper she'd signed just a few minutes earlier.

"I thought I was signing to Anna and Alf's marriage, not my own."

"Oh, God, Eldri. I thought you understood what was going on. I thought you liked me. After all, you did agree to marry me."

"The paperwork and the vows were all in English, which you know I do not understand. You have played a mean trick on me, Ole Larsen, and you need to fix it."

"I'm sorry, Eldri, but it's not so easy to undo a marriage. The judge has gone home, and we should, too."

"The only *home* I will let you take me is back to Mrs. Brotvik's."

"But Eldri, you hate it there. And without Anna, you'll hate it even more. The only reason you need to go back to Mrs. Brotvik's now is to collect your things and then come home with me."

"Home to where, Ole? That smelly logging camp? I do not think so. In fact, if I had any other way of getting back to Conway, I would take it. But, thanks to you, I am stuck, and I want to go back."

Anna and Alf had shifted slightly away from Eldri and Ole, where they stood helplessly by and watched the tense exchange.

"You told me Eldri had agreed to marry Ole today," Anna whispered through gritted teeth as she gave her new husband a light poke in the ribs.

"Well, Anna, that's what I thought."

"You *thought*? Oh, Alf. We've made a huge mistake."

"No, Anna. This is not our fault. We both thought Eldri knew what was happening. I don't know how Ole could do something so stupid."

"It may not be *all* our fault, Alf, but we share some of the blame for not doing a better job of looking out for our friend. What are we going to do about it?"

Alf looked into the eyes of his new wife and, in a rare moment of certitude, told her, "You know what, Anna? This is between Eldri and Ole. It has nothing to do with us, and I won't have it turn into our first fight as a married couple. It's our wedding day, too, and we deserve to be happy about it."

Eldri overheard what Alf said and realized he was right. She might have been tricked into getting married today, but Alf and Anna had not. They had waited a long time for this special day, and Eldri realized it would be wrong to let what Ole had done ruin it for her best friends.

Taking a deep breath, Eldri looped her arm around Ole's and said, "We will figure this out," then guided him over to where Anna and Alf were standing. "This is a big day, for all of us, and we should be celebrating," she continued, with as much enthusiasm as she could summon. She hoped it sounded convincing.

Confused, but hugely relieved, Ole squeezed Eldri's arm affectionately, "Yes, let's."

At the hotel in Mount Vernon, the two couples sat down to a delicious dinner in its elegant dining room—a rare treat.

Smiling, Anna said, "This is all so wonderful, but I'm just happy not to be eating dinner at Mrs. Brotvik's, after we had served it, of course. And, not only that, we'd have had to cook it and clean up after. Isn't that right, Eldri?"

Eldri could only nod because, as much as she hated Brotvik's, on this night she couldn't wait to get back there. Every bite of her food tasted like sawdust.

When dinner and conversation came to an end, the couples drove back to Fir Island and the land Alf had bought with Ole a few years ago. Anna's wedding night would be spent in the one-room log cabin Alf had hurriedly built, with Ole's help, after Anna had accepted his proposal. When they arrived, Alf announced, "Well, here we are, my dear wife, our honeymoon castle." He swept Anna up in his arms and carried her over the threshold—the very, very modest threshold. It wasn't much, but it was theirs, and it was home—at least for now. The happy couple waved good night to Ole and Eldri and closed the cabin's door.

CHAPTER 3

Without Alf and Anna's natural gaiety, the barge ride across the Skagit to Conway was a quiet one. Ole figured it was because Eldri was probably pretty tired. After all, it had been a long and very eventful day. When Ole stopped the wagon in front of Mrs. Brotvik's, he lightly touched her arm. "I'll come back tomorrow morning and help you collect your things."

"That will be fine," Eldri replied, with less enthusiasm than Ole had expected. Nevertheless, he jumped out of the wagon, went over to Eldri's side, and helped her down. He'd have liked to kiss his new wife good night, but he hesitated, just for a moment, and the opportunity was lost. Eldri was already up the steps and letting herself inside the boardinghouse. Without turning around, she closed the door. "Goodbye, Ole," she whispered, quietly enough that he didn't hear.

Finally alone, Eldri tried to focus her thoughts. First of all, she was mad at Ole. In fact, she didn't recall ever being as angry as she was now. She could not believe she had been so fooled, especially by someone she thought she could trust. America, "The Land of Opportunity," indeed. Ya, sure, it was the Land of Opportunity all right—for those waiting to take advantage of the latest dumb immigrant to step onto her shores.

It wasn't as though she didn't like Ole. She liked him just fine, better than fine, in fact. And she was flattered by the smiles he sent her way in town, at the boardinghouse, and in church. But she wanted to pick the time and place she would be married, and who she would marry. Most of all, she wanted to *know* she was being married.

It wasn't until the early morning hours that Eldri finally drifted into a restless sleep. But at least by then, she had figured out what to do.

Ole was up early and excited for what he expected would be another best day. After he'd washed and finished dressing inside the bunkhouse, he went over to the camp's barn and again hitched his horses to the wagon. He felt as though he'd only just unhitched them. But early as it was, the pair of old reliables was ready to go, and so was Ole. He decided to leave Gus at the camp again. The other loggers would take care of her, and Ole had a big day ahead of him.

The sky was gray, a sloppy rain was falling, and Ole was glad he'd left the canopy on the wagon last night. But he cared nothing about the bleak weather. After all, he was on his way to pick up his bride and start a new life with her. Ole couldn't believe his good luck. He'd been a little worried after the ceremony. Eldri seemed pretty upset with him, but the dinner afterward with Alf and Anna had been a wonderful time. And the ride alone with Eldri back to Mrs. Brotvik's so filled his heart that he thought it might burst.

Everything changed, though, when Ole got to the boardinghouse.

"She's not here," was all Mrs. Brotvik said when she opened the door after Ole's excited knock.

"What do you mean, she's not here? I dropped her here just last night. She knew I was coming to get her this morning."

"I don't know what you did, Mr. Larsen, but whatever it was, she left, and I'm quite certain it is your fault."

Ole's heart sank. He now knew he'd made a terrible mistake. "I just didn't think that through," he said, not realizing he'd said it out loud.

"No, whatever *that* was, it seems you did not."

"Do you know where she's gone?"

Mrs. Brotvik stood mute.

Ole slumped down onto the front steps, pulled his cap back on his head, and put his face into his hands.

"Don't you do that, Ole Larsen. Get up, get up."

"Mrs. Brotvik, as hard-hearted as you are and as much as I'd like to accommodate you, I cannot get up just now. You will have to wait a moment. Did Eldri say anything to you?"

"Not much. She just came downstairs this morning, bag in hand, and said goodbye. I was so shocked I couldn't speak. But I was pretty mad, I tell you."

"I'm sure you were," Ole replied. He did not add, Because you are always mad.

"Ya, and with good reason. So I went upstairs into her room. Sure enough, all her things were gone. The only belongings left in there are Anna's. When I came back downstairs, I saw Eldri had left me a letter on the table here in the entryway."

"What does it say?"

"You think I'll tell you? No sir. The letter was addressed to me, and I'm not sharing its contents with you, or anyone else. She left a second letter, though. It has your name on it."

"What? Why didn't you say so?"

"Because you didn't ask."

"Have you finished reading it?" Ole said spitefully.

"I most certainly have not."

"You have not *finished* reading it, or you have not read it?" Ole couldn't help himself.

"I have not read your letter. Here, take it and go. Because of you and that friend of yours. Alf? Ya, that's right, Alf, I've lost my two best workers."

Ole was finally able to stand. He took the letter from the hand Mrs. Brotvik had thrust at him, turned around, and climbed back into his wagon. He probably should have thanked Mrs. Brotvik for giving him the letter, however reluctantly she'd done it, but he couldn't. She was too mean, he was too hurt, and he was out of charity.

Then, having nothing better to do, Ole drove the wagon over to Red's Tavern.

"Want an Oly, Ole?" the owner bartender asked, thinking himself very clever.

"Very funny, Red, but I'm not in the mood."

When Red handed the cold Olympia draft to Ole, he also took a good look at the face of the man across the bar from him and asked, "What's the matter with you, Ole? You look like you lost your last friend."

Ole answered him, "I feel like I've lost my last friend."

"Want to talk about it?"

"Nope."

Red knew when to quit, and he said nothing more.

Steeling himself with a long swallow of the cold beer, Ole opened Eldri's letter.

September 1, 1908

Dear Ole,

I thought I liked you, but now I wonder. Maybe you let yourself believe I knew what was

*happening at the courthouse, but I assure you I
did not. The fact is, you made a fool of me. No
one likes to be made the fool, and I certainly
expected I would know when I was being wed.*

*I will not be going with you to the logging camp,
or anywhere else. My home is where I say it is
until I say it is not. I thought my home was in
Conway, but you took that away from me
yesterday. I do not want to see you right now,
and I do not know if that feeling will last for a
little while or forever. But I do know I have to
leave in order to figure it out.*

*This is my life, Ole Larsen, and I will decide who
I will spend it with.*

Sincerely,

Eldri Holm

Without thinking, Ole crumpled Eldri's letter, then thought
better of it and tried to straighten the wrinkles on the damp
bar, smearing some of the ink. "Shit. Another beer, Red."

After drinking himself one, or a few, too many, Ole
stumbled out the door and onto the street. It had started

raining again, of course. "God bless it, does it always have to be so damned muddy?" Ole asked no one. Just then, he slipped and fell, hard, into the sodden street. He looked up toward Heaven. "Well, that is just fine, then. I guess this is your way of saying 'yes'?"

After a couple of futile attempts, a wobbly Ole finally managed to pull himself up out of the muck and, despite the haze he was in, could tell that cleaning himself up was hopeless. He didn't need to be sober in order to know he needed a bath. Staggering over to the wagon, he pulled out the waxed cotton bag he kept under the seat. Fortunately, Ole always kept a dry change of clothes inside that bag, but they were intended to be used in the event of a sudden Pacific Northwest rain shower, not a drunken roll in a wet and filthy street.

The little brass bell at the top of the barbershop door jingled, loudly enough to announce Ole's arrival. Looking up from his newspaper, the barber simply burst out laughing, "What have you gone and done, Ole? You are truly a sight to see."

"Shut up and fill me a tub," Ole slurred in response.

"Okay, okay. Jesus, Ole, you don't need to be such a jerk about it."

"Yeah, you're right. Sorry."

The hot bath helped Ole sober up and collect his thoughts. He began to realize there was nothing for him to do but wait and hope that he'd not forever ruined his chance of a life with Eldri. It was he, Ole, who had made the mistake, and it was up to Eldri to forgive him. All he could do now was try to make himself worthy of her return. After getting cleaned up, and leaving a big tip at the barbershop, the sad man drove his wagon back to the logging camp.

The next morning, Ole awoke with the thick head he deserved from having that one, or a few, too many at Red's. And, as if things weren't bad enough, while he was gone, someone at the camp had fed the wrong thing to Gus. Although she was just about the best dog in the world, she also had probably the world's worst digestive system. Sometimes he thought Gus wasn't short for "Augusta." It was short for "Disgusting." Her silent flatulence could clear a room.

"Aw, Gus, what did you eat? That is about the worst smell you've put out in, well, ever. Or maybe my head is so big I'm just smelling it more. No matter, you need to get outside. Go on. Out!" Ole snapped his fingers and pointed toward the door. A forlorn Gus gave Ole her best pitiful look, stuck her tail between her legs, and crept outside while Ole sat on the edge of his bunk, rubbed his hands through his hair, then settled them over his eyes.

On that same morning, when Ole was waking up with
nothing but excitement for the day ahead, a miserable and
exhausted Eldri was waking up, too. Despite her misery and
exhaustion, she forced herself out of bed and packed her bag.

When Eldri said goodbye, Mrs. Brotvik put up a fuss
about Anna leaving and now Eldri. But her complaints fell
on deaf ears. Eldri didn't care; she knew it wouldn't be long
before there were two new immigrant girls knocking on Mrs.
Brotvik's door in need of a room and work. Times were hard
in Norway, very hard, and she was losing many of her young
people to the hope of finding better lives in America.
Besides, Eldri also knew Anna had given Mrs. Brotvik
plenty of notice and there had been more than enough time
to hire someone to replace her. Eldri gave Mrs. Brotvik her
sister's address in Seattle but waited until the grumbling
woman left the room to place the two letters she'd written
the night before on the entryway table. Then, picking up her
bag, she walked wearily out the door.

Eldri had decided she would stay with her sister, Marta,
at least for a while. She knew she was walking away from
some big challenges and toward others. But there was
nowhere else to go. And, welcomed by her sister or not, it
didn't matter. As much as Eldri felt she belonged in
Conway, sadly, she also felt no choice but to leave it.

While waiting at the depot, Eldri finally realized she was
as angry with herself as she was with Ole. She had been so

determined to make her own way, to set the course for her own life. It was, after all, a large part of the reason she'd left Norway, crossed the Atlantic, endured the humiliations of Ellis Island, and finally settled all the way across America. But in the end, she had failed. And all because she'd not learned enough English to know she was getting married. How stupid could one immigrant be?

"Paper, miss?"

Eldri knew she had to watch every nickel, especially now, but after buying the ticket that would take her south to Seattle, she also bought herself a copy of *The Skagit News* from the young boy who had approached her, hawking the local paper on the wooden platform. Her determination to learn English, and not to be fooled again, outweighed her need for thrift. She figured learning to read the newspaper was as good a place, and this day as good a time, to start as any. But when she sat down and opened the paper, the words were just a blur and she soon felt the familiar pain of a headache coming on, threatening her already fragile composure.

Fatigue can be just as compelling as determination, however, especially determination that's being sabotaged by an aching head. Once on the train, despite the jostling, the noise, and the smoke, Eldri was soon lulled into a light sleep. As she dozed, her dreams were filled with memories of the farm in Norway and how like her native country Conway had felt. When she'd first arrived, Eldri could not believe there was another place in the world so like Rissa. It was small wonder that so many Norwegians settled in the Skagit Valley, which made it easy—too easy, in fact—not to bother learning English. You just didn't need it, unless, of course, you were going to be a witness at your best friend's marriage at the local courthouse—or you wanted to know you were getting married, too.

A high-pitched, whining voice startled her awake. "Tickets, tickets, please." After fumbling around in her bag, to the annoyance of the impatient conductor, Eldri tried giving him a friendly smile. But he simply took the ticket, pierced it with his metal punch, handed it back to her most officiously and continued his way down the aisles of the passenger cars. "Tickets, tickets, please." Ah well, at least she understood that much English. Small consolation.

After spending what seemed forever shaking from side to side, Eldri felt the train slowing down. It was arriving at the depot in Ballard, the northwest Seattle neighborhood where Marta lived. To Eldri's relief, the autumn sky had cleared, and the day had warmed. It would make the climb up the hill to Marta's house somewhat easier, and certainly more pleasant, than dodging rain and slogging through mud. Eldri might have been willing to part with a nickel for a newspaper, but there was no reason she couldn't walk a few blocks and save herself the streetcar fare.

Looking around, Eldri was amazed by all the building going on around her. Marta had written about Seattle's growth, but no letter could describe what she was seeing with her own eyes. It was both exciting and intimidating. Before she could take it all in, though, Eldri was standing in front of a huge, three-story house with the same address as those on Marta's letters. She walked up the steps to the landing and the screened-in front porch of the grandest house she had ever seen.

CHAPTER 4

Could this be right? A small brass plaque mounted above
the doorbell confirmed that indeed it was. "Holm House."
Eldri ran her fingers over the name, drew in a deep breath,
and rang the bell.

The door was opened by a boy of about fifteen. "Yes?"

"Uhm, Marta Holm is here?" Eldri struggled to ask in
English.

"Maaaaybe," the boy said.

"She is here?"

"I'll go see," and he shut the door.

Well, that was very strange. Eldri turned around to look
at the street. In the front window of one of the houses across
the street, she saw a curtain slowly crack open, then close
with a deliberate snap. Also, very strange.

"Eldri?" said a familiar voice.

Marta was standing at the threshold with her arms open
wide. Unlike Eldri, who was petite and brunette, Marta
looked like many Norwegians: tall and blonde. Statuesque
would be the one word to best describe her. The sisters
might not have shared their stature or hair color, but what
they did share was the same piercing, pale blue eyes.

At last, thought Eldri, who was so very tired, in both

body and spirit, that she nearly fell into her sister's embrace.

Marta took Eldri's arm and guided her into a lavish parlor. The room was furnished with two overstuffed sofas and four matching armchairs, all covered in a rich, cream-colored silk brocade. A beautiful Oriental rug in muted shades of purple, blue, and red covered the floor. The heavy drapes, of the same brocade as on the furniture, closed the room off entirely from the world outside. She saw an upright grand piano of dark mahogany gracing the far corner of the room and a stunning rose-colored glass chandelier hanging over the dining room table, catching the early evening's light.

"Well, what do you think?" Marta asked.

"What is this place, Marta?"

"This is a boardinghouse, but it's a boardinghouse with very special tenants."

Eldri's eyes got wide. "Oh no, Marta, you are not?"

"Don't worry, Eldri. No, I'm not a whore. But I am a successful businesswoman. And this is a rather unique establishment."

Her world had now fully turned upside down, and Eldri's confusion was complete. First yesterday with Ole, and now today with Marta. Is nothing as it seems to be? Her nose started stinging, and she felt tears welling in her eyes.

Again, Marta took her sister by the arm and led her into

the kitchen. She pulled up a chair by the stove. "Sit. I'll make us some tea. I'm rather certain there's a reason, a very big reason, you've suddenly come all the way down from Conway. Tell me."

After a few minutes, the familiar warmth of a cup of tea in her hands and her sister's sympathetic look comforted Eldri and somewhat emboldened her. She wiped her wet eyes and told Marta about her wedding day. When she finished, Marta couldn't stifle a chuckle. "Well, I just cannot believe it."

"If I had wanted to be laughed at, Marta, I could have stayed where I was."

"Oh, now, don't be so proud. I'm not laughing at you. Well, not exactly. Think about it, Elle. Doesn't that sound so typical of the men we left behind? Ever the practical ones, those Norwegian men. I tell you, I don't miss them—not one bit. And besides, have you taken a good look at yourself lately?"

"No. That is not something I am in the habit of doing."

"Well, you should. And if you did, you would see a lovely young woman with a welcoming smile and kindness in her lovely blue eyes. If this Ole is any kind of man, Norwegian or no, he also sees a healthy, strong woman who would likely bear him a family of equally healthy, strong children. And just look at those perfect white teeth," Marta joked.

"You make me sound like a cow."

"Oh, Elle. Seriously, why would this man not try to marry you at the earliest opportunity?"

"Be that as it may, Marta, I am not having it. I am not. My body and my life are my own, and I am not going to be tricked into giving them away."

"Don't misunderstand me, little sister. I'm on your side. I don't give my body away freely, and I will never give away my life. But enough of that for now. Elle, you look so very tired. I would guess there wasn't much sleep for you last night."

"Almost none."

Marta said, "There's a room up in the attic. It's not big, but it's quiet and warm. I think you'll be comfortable there. After you're rested, we'll make a plan."

Too tired to argue and without any better idea, Eldri let Marta lead her up to the small attic room. It was nothing like the rest of the house. There was a simple, metal-framed double bed with a yellow chenille spread covering it, an oak nightstand with a marble top, a low, tiger-oak dresser with a washing pitcher and bowl sitting on top and an oval mirror hanging on the wall above it. There was a rag rug on the floor that looked like the ones their mother used to make to cover the cold floors in Rissa.

"There is a bathroom downstairs, off the kitchen, that you can use."

"Inside?"

"Yes, Elle, inside." Marta smiled.

"Ah, heaven."

Eldri thought she would never be able to stop the jumble of thoughts spinning around in her head, but exhaustion got the better of her, and she was soon hard asleep. As on the train, her dreams were filled with memories of life back in Norway. But these dreams were of the times when she and Marta were small, when Far and Mor were still alive and when her brother, Jan, had not yet turned heartless.

The sound of lively piano music broke the reverie of Eldri's dreams. Whoever was playing the instrument, which Eldri assumed was the upright grand in Marta's parlor, certainly had a gift. She dragged herself out of the cozy bed and was surprised to see it had gotten dark outside. How long had she been asleep?

Someone—Marta, she supposed—had put fresh water in the white porcelain pitcher and left a clean towel next to it. Eldri was grateful for the gesture and felt much better after washing her face and hands and repinning her hair back into its usual bun at the nape of her slender neck. When she felt ready to face the world again, Eldri retraced the steps she had taken a few hours earlier.

As she entered the parlor for the second time that day, the scene she came upon took her breath away. Before her stood four elegantly dressed women, her sister among them, and, standing alongside, three distinguished-looking gentlemen. At the piano sat the boy who had opened the door for her earlier in the day.

"Elle, there you are." The music abruptly stopped, and Eldri found herself being stared at by several pairs of strangers' eyes. She, who had never been very good at hiding her feelings, was sure everyone in the room could tell what she was thinking, which she admitted rather guiltily to herself, wasn't very nice. Then she watched Marta glide across the elegant room toward her.

Had Marta been telling Eldri the truth about being only a "successful businesswoman" and nothing more? Oh, God, I hope so, thought Eldri.

Marta clapped her hands to draw the group's attention. "Everyone, everyone, let me introduce my baby sister, Eldri. She's come down from Conway to visit me. She didn't quite expect to find me in such august company," Marta said, dramatically sweeping an arm around the room as she did so. "I know you will all do your best to make her feel at home."

"August?" Eldri wondered. Her own name, Eldri, and the word, August, were the only words she'd recognized in her sister's introduction. But it wasn't August. Why had Marta said it was? Eldri realized her English lessons couldn't start too soon. There was so much to learn. It made her dizzy.

One by one, the elegantly dressed women and the distinguished-looking gentlemen greeted Eldri, until Marta announced it was time for dinner. Eldri couldn't understand much of what they said, but she had to admit their words certainly seemed warm and sincere, enough so that Eldri found herself feeling a flicker of hope that her life might right itself again. Whatever *right* now meant.

Eldri followed the group, and the wonderful smells, into the dining room. She realized she hadn't eaten since last night's fateful dinner, and she was famished. The table was decorated with a beautiful, white hardanger-embroidered runner, one of Marta's tributes to her Norwegian heritage, and slim white tapers in sterling candlesticks, their flames casting a warm, pink glow on the chandelier prisms that had reflected the sun so brilliantly earlier in the day. The food was plentiful, hearty and warm, as was the conversation around the table. Marta patiently translated much of what was being said, and Eldri could feel herself gradually relaxing. Was it really just yesterday that she had been at the courthouse in Mount Vernon?

When all had finished dining, they excused themselves and either retreated to the parlor or upstairs to their private rooms. Tommy, the door greeter and pianist, came out of the kitchen and started clearing the dishes from the table.

"Tommy, would you ask your mother to come in here, please?" asked Marta.

"Sure, Miss Marta."

The woman who came out of the kitchen looked nothing

like the others Eldri had just met. She looked more like the women Eldri knew up in Conway. Her rather round body was covered in a modest cotton day dress, and she looked, well, real.

"You needin' somethin', Marta?" the woman asked while drying her wet hands on the skirt of her well-worn apron.

"No, no, Mary. I just wanted to introduce my sister, Eldri. She'll be staying with us for a while." In Norwegian, Marta told her sister that Mary Miller was in charge, very much in charge, of the kitchen.

"Hello, Mary Miller."

"A pleasure, Eldri," Mary Miller said, holding out her still damp hand to Eldri's. Then, as quickly as she'd come into the dining room, Mary excused herself, "If you don't mind, Marta, I've a lot to finish up in the kitchen."

"Of course, Mary." Marta then turned to her sister, "Now it's time for us to talk." Although somewhat intimidated by the serious tone, Eldri couldn't have agreed more.

"Marta, who are these people? They seem so in their own world and yet so like everyone else. I do not understand."

"Well, Elle, life can be hard sometimes, especially for women and the men who love them, and their choices in it can be limited."

"But you could have stayed on with me in Conway. It is lots of nice folks there. I go to a good church and work in the boardinghouse. Well, never mind about the boardinghouse.

You already know Mrs. Brotvik is not so nice, but most other folks are."

"Eldri, I know many nice folks, too, and as for church, well, I was never much for that, anyway. Don't misunderstand me. I like my life. It's never dull, and it serves a certain purpose. If I had wanted to live in the country, I could have stayed in Norway. No, I'd rather be here. I can't imagine a life of serving lunch to a bunch of boorish loggers."

"That is not fair, Marta. There are many fine men up in Conway and on Fir Island, loggers included," Eldri said, a bit more defensively than she'd intended.

"Oh, I know, I know, don't be so sensitive. Or ... wait ... maybe there's a reason for your sensitivity."

"No, it is just that . . ."

"Is it possible you like that new husband of yours more than you care to admit?"

"No, Marta, it is not."

"Ah well, let's leave that for now. Tell me, what are you going to do tomorrow?"

"The truth is, I have no idea. What *am* I going to do tomorrow?"

"Well, while you were resting, I had a chance to give it some thought. You are welcome to stay here, but I must tell you this is a house without judgment. And if you do choose to stay, you need to understand that. You see, and you say, nothing. These folks all have their real lives and their pretend lives. This house is part of the pretend."

"I understand, Marta."

"Perhaps so, but you still need to think about it."

"I will, but the first thing I need to think about is finding work. What to do? I am certain I do not want to keep serving coffee and fish soup. Brotvik's sure taught me that. Sewing, maybe? We both I know I have a talent for it. Maybe I should advertise myself as a seamstress."

Once again, Marta let out a laugh, and Eldri was growing tired of it. "This is funny?"

"Sorry, Elle. It's just, here in Seattle you don't exactly want to advertise that you're a seamstress, not to mention a talented one. The women who do, well, they don't actually *sew*, not with a needle and thread anyway. If that's what you decide you want to do, you'll need to use another word. Dressmaker is better."

Eldri's head was beginning to ache, and another of her nagging headaches threatened.

Marta caught her sister's pained look and softened her tone. "Don't worry so much, Elle, you're a smart girl. You just don't know about life here in Seattle, but it won't take you long. Be patient. I suggest you go back upstairs and get yourself a good night's sleep. You'll feel better tomorrow. Remember Mor telling us things always look better in the light of day? She was right, you know."

"Thank you, Marta. Good night." Eldri hugged her sister, hard, then dragged herself upstairs once again and embraced the calm of the night.

CHAPTER 5

On her first morning in Seattle, Eldri looked out the window of her attic room at a view that could not have been more different from the one she had become accustomed to at Mrs. Brotvik's. "Now what, girl?" she asked herself.

After getting dressed for the day, she went downstairs, tempted by the smell of freshly brewed coffee. The coffee at Mrs. Brotvik's certainly never tempted. Bitter and weak, all it did was help warm one's chilled bones first thing in the morning. Eldri reached the bottom step just in time to see Marta in her dressing gown kissing a man with a passion reserved only for a woman deeply in love. She tried to slip into the kitchen without being noticed.

"Sit down," Mary said when she saw Eldri walking into the kitchen. "Coffee?" she asked as she held up the pot for Eldri to see.

"Coffee, ya, please ... Mary?"

"Aye, that's me, Mary Miller. It's lovely you're here, lass." Mary poured the fresh coffee into a cup and handed it to a confused-looking Eldri.

"Oh, sorry, dearie. I forgot. No English."

True, Eldri understood little of what Mary said, but she had already resolved to correct that. She finally had reasons—many good reasons—to learn English. "Mary, I am sorry. I do not understand much."

"That's okay. We'll just have to work on it," Mary said with a kind wink.

The coffee tasted as delicious as its aroma had promised. Eldri wrapped her chilled hands around the cup and looked into the steaming liquid. She thought about this sister she had shared a bed with—as well as all her secrets—until just over a year ago. Now there were so many new secrets.

"Penny for *dine tanker*," Marta greeted Eldri as she walked into the kitchen.

"Oh, good morning, Marta. What did you say?"

"Penny for your thoughts. It's a common saying in America."

"People get paid to tell what they are thinking? That makes no sense."

"Silly girl," Marta said. "It's not serious. It's just a way of asking what you were thinking about so deeply when I came in."

"Ah, ya. 'Penny for your thoughts.' I think I will want to remember that." Eldri smiled.

Marta took the coffee Mary had poured for her and sat down next to Eldri. "Thank you, Mary."

"Welcome, Marta. Anythin' else for now? If not, I'll get back to dumpin' this chicken into the stew pot."

"No, we're fine, thanks." Then Marta turned to Eldri

and, in Norwegian, said, "Let's leave Mary to her work and go into the dining room. I'd like to tell you about the folks who live here. And I'll trust you to keep what I say to yourself."

"Ya, sure. I will."

Once resettled, Marta took a long swallow of coffee, momentarily savored the taste of the dark liquid, then began her narrative by telling Eldri about Harry and Florence in Room One.

"They met over thirty years ago at a New Year's Gala. Just imagine, Elle, what the town of Seattle must have been like in its early days before the big fire. Harry and Florence's attraction was immediate, they both felt it, but they were also both married to other people. Florence says she allowed herself to acknowledge the attraction, but she never acted on it. Years later, though, when Harry learned Florence had been widowed, he took a chance and reacquainted himself with her.

"Harry is still very married, but as far as Florence is concerned, how Harry conducts himself in his own marriage is his business. So when Harry invited her, Florence agreed to move in here. They enjoy each other's company as often as the opportunity presents itself. They're quite social and glad their time together isn't wasted looking over their shoulders or spent hiding in Florence's room. They especially enjoy gathering with the rest of us around the dinner table.

"From what I understand, Florence's husband was much in control, and I think she appreciates the freedom of her new life. She is loved, and yet she can finally do exactly what she wants, when she wants. Florence and her husband had no children, and she has no other family. Without Harry, I think Florence would be very, very lonely."

"Oh, Marta, can you imagine waiting thirty years for love?"

"Well, we do what we must. But, it is nice they can finally be together."

"And then there's Cissy, who lives in Room Two. She's in her early twenties and is rather silly and frivolous. She's a little clumsy, too. I think sometimes her feet get ahead of the rest of her body.

"Perhaps she will slow down when she gets a little older?"

"Maybe, Elle, but she's older than you are, and it hasn't happened yet. Anyway, Cissy first caught the attention of Albert while she was working as a server at the Swedish Club downtown. Albert is a widower and many years Cissy's senior. In fact, Albert's own children are older than Cissy.

"So, Cissy must be married, and that's why they cannot be together?"

"She is not, Elle."

"Then why do they not marry?"

"Well, there is the fact that Cissy is so much younger

than Albert, and his children will never believe she loves
him for anything but his money. Another, and perhaps
greater, complication is that Cissy has some Negro in her.
Her grandmother was a slave in the state of Louisiana
before this country's civil war."

"A slave? Truly?"

"Yes, Elle, a slave. A shameful chapter in this country's
history."

"But Cissy doesn't look Negro."

"In this country, you don't have to *look* Negro, or have
more than a drop of Negro in your blood, in order to be
counted as *all* Negro. Albert loved his wife, and when she
died he felt part of himself had died with her. Cissy has
made him laugh again when he thought he never would. She
brings all the joy Albert has in his life. But his children will
never know that because Albert realizes they would never be
able to see past Cissy's age or her lineage. For all her
silliness, Cissy has not a mean bone in her body. People
often overlook that in her. Albert saw it right away. Theirs
is a bittersweet story."

Eldri nodded in agreement.

"Harald rents Room Three. Although his business is
headquartered in Chicago, it often requires him to travel to
Seattle. He has a wife who loves him, and four wonderful
children. He says he, in turn, loves his wife, but he admits it
is difficult, impossible really, for him to stay faithful to just

one woman. So he takes much advantage of his travels to Seattle. Harald is charming and rich, and despite his roving eye, he's actually quite kind. He keeps a permanent room here, but not so a permanent relationship. One lady after another comes—but soon goes. He lets his ladies go as gently as he can, but he always lets them go. There are times, though, when Harald relishes some quiet, and he'll stay alone here for the whole of his visit."

"Well, it certainly sounds like he is an interesting man."

"Again, I say, Harald is very charming. Remember that, Elle," Marta said, cautioning her sister.

"I understand, Marta."

"Good."

Marta continued. "Susannah rents the last one, Room Four. Until a few years ago, she had a 'boardinghouse' of her own. The kind you worried I had, little sister."

Eldri blushed but said nothing.

"She owned a place called the Rose House in Portland. Do you know of Portland? It's a city about 200 miles south of here and just across the state line in Oregon."

Eldri nodded.

"Anyway, Rose House was decorated with lots of deep red silk and sparsely clad women, and it was very profitable."

"Why was it called the Rose House?" asked Eldri.

"Portland is known as the Rose City," answered Marta.

"Ah, very clever. And yet, if her business was so profitable, why did she leave it?"

"Susannah told me the day finally came when she decided she'd been raided one time too many, and she was simply too old anymore to sleep on a stiff jailhouse bunk, even if it was for only one night. So she sold the business to one of the ladies who worked for her and came north to Seattle, where she knew no one and no one knew her.

"Among Susannah's favorite pastimes is dressing in one of her best gowns, pinning on the biggest and fanciest hat she owns—and believe me, Elle, it is indeed big and truly fancy—stepping out onto the sidewalk and opening her lace parasol. With a smile on rouged lips, Susannah crosses the street and saunters past our nosy neighbor's house, turns to the window and nods slightly, then continues on her way. Of course, she knows the neighbor, Mrs. Jorvig, will be peering out that window, because she's always peering out. It brings Susannah a devilish glee to stir up Mrs. Jorvig and make her wonder what kind of house I'm running here."

"Shame on you, Marta."

"Me? I've done nothing wrong. Blame Susannah," Marta smiled. "Elle, every town, every neighborhood has those people who can't stand not knowing everything about everyone. And when there are gaps, they just fill them in with their own imaginations, which is usually how rumors get started. Mrs. Jorvig is the mistress of rumors in this neighborhood."

"When I arrived yesterday, I saw a curtain crack open, then suddenly snap shut."

"Was that in the house right across the street?"

"Ya, it was."

"Then, Elle, you've already met Mrs. Jorvig."

"We did not actually *meet*, Marta."

"What you got yesterday was about as much meeting as you'll ever get out of Mrs. Jorvig. She has watched the comings and goings of this house for years. But she became especially interested after Mrs. Halverson sold it to me. I'm sure she wonders where I got the money to buy this big house. I first saw her peering through those curtains when she watched every piece of furniture, the drapes, and the rugs being delivered. She doesn't like all the trees, but I'm sure that's because they block her view, which makes me appreciate them all the more. Her unwelcome behavior didn't start when I bought the house, though. She's had a harsh, and rather mean-spirited, opinion about this place for years. In fact, I've been told that she says to anyone who will listen, 'Seems like someone is always dying in there. I wouldn't step foot on the porch, not in a million years. Who knows what diseases that place carries? People go in and they come out in a box. With all those trees, I'll bet it's damp and smelly, too. No, I wouldn't want to go near that great big house. Not that I believe in ghosts, but if such things did exist, that's just the house they'd be looking for.' She carries on so.'"

"What's she talking about, Marta? Who died?"

"Well, Mrs. Halverson told me the first owner left his family somewhere back East, while he established a new business in Seattle and had the house built. Sadly, not long after moving his wife and six children here, he fell ill. He probably already had his suspicions, but I'm sure the blood on his handkerchief confirmed them. When his cough started, it was probably very slight and not of concern. But when it persists, as his did, you eventually figure out you won't be getting better. It wasn't very long before he was gone, and his family was back where they had come from. The house stood empty for years.

"Charlie Halverson eventually bought this house from the original owner's estate. Much like that man, Charlie, too, had planned to live a long life here with his wife and raise their family. But Charlie collapsed on the floor of the shingle mill a few years after he bought the place. Mrs. Halverson—Sally—still owned the house when I came to Ballard. She is a nice lady, and she worked very hard for her children after their father died. This house was well run, and it provided a good living for the Halversons. Sally said she never regretted not befriending Mrs. Jorvig, had that even been possible. Simply put, she thought it disrespectful to talk about the man who had built her house, and her own husband, in the way that she does, so she simply avoided the woman."

"I don't blame her," said Eldri.

"Nor I, Elle."

As if on cue, Susannah came walking into the kitchen. "Good morning, ladies."

"Good morning, Susannah. And how is Mrs. Jorvig today?" asked Marta.

"Fine as ever," Susannah replied with a broad grin and a twirl of her open parasol.

Eldri needed little translation to understand what Susannah had said. Her gestures were translation enough. "Is it always so interesting here?"

"Not always, Elle, but often enough."

After Susannah left the room, Eldri asked, "And ... who lives on the third floor?"

"Well, that's me, of course."

"You, ...and who else?" Eldri told Marta what she'd seen at the front door.

Marta smiled, "Ah, that was John, my business partner."

"Some strange business I saw," Eldri replied.

Marta's eyes got small, and her face tightened.

Eldri felt a harsh response forming. "Penny for your thoughts, Marta." Eldri smiled.

Marta's expression softened. "You about had me started, Elle."

"Ya, I could see that, and I apologize. I only meant to tease you a little. So, tell me about this *business partner* of yours."

"Another time, Elle. I've told you enough for now. And we both have things to do. I need to get back to running this house. And you, dear sister, need to figure out how you're going to fill your days."

No matter what he tried, Ole could not get his mind off Eldri. She was the best thing to have happened in his life. He'd had a chance at true happiness, but when Eldri left him, happiness left him, too. Worse, it was his own doing. How could he have been so stupid as to think Eldri would have the same strong feelings for him that he had for her?

Ole finally realized he would have no peace of his own until he made peace with Eldri. When he'd shown up that awful morning to fetch her, he'd gotten the feeling Mrs. Brotvik knew where Eldri had gone, but she was as stubborn as they come—even a little hateful—and had said nothing. So, once again, Ole hitched up the horses to his wagon and made the trip from the logging camp into Conway.

Ole's knock on the boardinghouse door was answered with no cordiality. "You, again? Do not keep pestering me, Mr. Larsen, you hear? Believe me, I'm not beyond going to the police about you."

"I've done nothing for you to go to the police about, Mrs. Brotvik. I'm here for only one reason: to find out where Eldri has gone. I'm sure you know, and if you had told me the last time I was here, I would not be back today."

"Fine, then. Wait here." Mrs. Brotvik slammed the front door in Ole's face. When he heard the click of the deadbolt, he could do nothing but sigh and shake his head.

The door flew open as abruptly as it had slammed. "Here!" Mrs. Brotvik threw out her arm and waved a scrap of paper at Ole. "Now, go! And do not bother me again. There is nothing else I can tell you."

Begging Mrs. Brotvik for the address was humiliating, but at least now Ole knew where Eldri had gone. He felt hopeless with words, but he had to do something. So as soon as he got back to the camp, Ole gathered his courage, lit the oil lamp on the stand next to his cot, scratched Gus's head for good luck and, using his best Norwegian, wrote Eldri the first of what would turn out to be many letters.

September 12, 1908

Dear Eldri,

I never thought I could make another person so mad as I did you.

I made the mistake of thinking you cared for me as much as I cared for you, and I thought we would have a good life together because the life you said you wanted at the picnic was just the one I, too, have hoped for. I now see how wrong I was.

The fact remains, though, we are legally married, and I don't know what to do about that.

Maybe you will not always stay so mad at me and will write to me sometime, if only to tell me you are safe.

Your husband,

Ole Larsen

Ole sealed the letter and put it in the post right away, knowing that if he waited, he would likely lose his nerve and it would stay stuffed in his back pocket.

CHAPTER 6

Grace's family would never be rich. They would never live up there on "The Hill," Capitol Hill, with the Yeslers, the Dennys, the Mercers, and all the other families who had streets named after them. But Grace and her parents were a family of simple needs, and as long as they were together, they were content. No, theirs wasn't a grand life, not even almost, but it was good enough for Grace and her parents.

Coming to Seattle was supposed to signal a fresh start. They'd heard that everywhere you went there was work to be found, in fishing, logging, and, of course, mining. Things weren't going too well for Da in Montana, so he and Ma—he never made a decision without Ma—decided to head farther west. But, as the saying goes, "The best laid plans of mice and men often go awry." It sure didn't take long for things to go awry, and for Da to realize he was too old to log or fish. And they'd left Montana so he could get away from the mines. Da was a good listener, though, and he'd always been able to pull a hearty draft. So he eventually found work at Murphy's Bar down on Ballard Avenue, serving up beer to the Swedish mill workers and the Norwegian fishermen. Murph also rented a couple of rooms above his bar to Grace's family, and while Da worked downstairs, Grace and Ma kept busy doing the washing for Murphy's.

Then it all fell apart. Da came upstairs feeling feverish and was gone within a week. Ma, thinking she was only exhausted from taking care of Da, was gone just a few days later. In less than a month, Grace went from being loved by the two most important people in her world to being an orphan.

Thankfully, Murph ignored the rumors about the sickness going around in his place and let Grace stay on in one of the upstairs rooms. The bar's business didn't suffer from the rumors for long. Good bars rarely do. But grateful as she was to Murph for keeping her on, Grace couldn't have been more miserable. Or so she thought.

Grace had also started working more and more downstairs in the kitchen, and eventually Murph had her going into to the new market at Pike Place, to collect fresh vegetables for the kitchen. Tommy Miller often went with her.

"Shouldn't you be in school, Tommy?"

"Naw, miss. I don't have much use for books. And besides, I'm too busy lookin' after you." He'd said with a smile.

But there were days when Tommy had other errands to run or his ma needed his help over at Miss Marta's house, which left Grace going alone to the market. And those were the days she would find Jack waiting for her when she got off the streetcar on her return. Jack's attention was flattering, which was perhaps the reason Grace never noticed that he came around only when Tommy didn't.

Grace knew who Jack was, or thought she did, because he was a regular at Murphy's Bar. With his curly black hair and stocky build, he didn't quite fit in among the tall, fair-haired Scandinavians, but he sure could drink with the best of them. He also had a wink and that smile, and a talent for making a girl feel she was something special.

"Carry your bags, Grace?"

"Thank you, Jack, but only if it doesn't take you out of your way."

"No, ma'am, you're exactly on my way."

And so it went, for several weeks.

But on that gray and drizzly morning in September, when Grace stepped off the streetcar and saw Jack waiting for her, she knew something wasn't right. Grace recognized the signs. Living above a bar, she'd seen that glazed look often enough. Jack was drunk. Really drunk. He sauntered, more like staggered, up to her as though intending to walk her back to Murphy's as usual. But this time was different, and Grace got a bad feeling that made her shiver.

"Hullo there, Grace. Want to hand me that bag? You cold? You look cold."

"Thanks, Jack, it's just a little damp today. I can manage the bag. I think you need to go home and sleep off whatever it is you've had to drink."

"What's the matter? Not good enough for you now?"

"No, Jack, it's not that. You just look all in."

"All in, you say? Well, ain't that rich? All in is *exactly* what I want, Grace." Jack laughed. "I think it's time for me to be showin' just how good I am for you. Something I've been wantin' to do for a long time." Jack grabbed Grace's arm, and her basket went flying. As the morning's produce scattered, Jack dragged Grace into the narrow alleyway behind the library.

The next morning, Grace was afraid to look in the tiny oval mirror above her dresser. When she did, she barely recognized the face staring back at her. During a fitful sleep, Grace had held out a faint hope that her encounter with Jack had just been a bad dream. But the truth was, she'd known better, and the face she saw in the mirror simply confirmed it.

Grace barely remembered getting back to Murphy's yesterday and up the stairs without being noticed, but sometime after dragging herself back to her room, Murph had knocked on her door.

"Grace, you in there?"

"Oh! Murph. I'm here."

"You okay? Did you go to the market? How come you

didn't show up in the kitchen?" Murph asked through the unopened door.

"I'm sorry, Murph, I'm sorry. I fell down hard on my way back. I think maybe I hit my head or something, and I lost my basket and the produce. It scattered all over in the mud."

"And you didn't let me know? Now we're gonna have to figure out something else for dinner. This isn't like you, Grace."

"I know, Murph. But I was hurting pretty bad when I got back. I needed to lie down. I guess I fell asleep. I'm really sorry."

"All right, all right, enough of the apologies. You okay? Maybe I should go get Doc?"

"No, I'm okay, or I will be. But can I have the rest of today off?"

"Yeah, sure. Don't worry about it."

"And, please, don't call Doc."

"I don't feel quite right about that, Grace, but I'll not force you."

Grace had shuddered when she heard the word *force*, but she managed to catch her breath and say, "Thanks, Murph."

"Sure Grace. Get some rest. But if you're not better by tomorrow, I will be calling Doc."

"I'll be better for sure," Grace had lied. She didn't think she'd ever be better again, but at some point, she had drifted back into that fitful sleep.

And now, assessing the damage, Grace saw her eyes were red and swollen, more from crying than anything else, and there was blood caked around her nose. Her lower lip was split and swollen, too. At least Jack hadn't broken any of her teeth. She didn't dare cry because her ribs hurt so badly she could hardly breathe, and crying would only make them hurt worse. Inside, she felt as though she'd been ripped right up her middle.

Grace was sore everywhere, no place more so than where Jack had forced himself inside her.

And that just added to the sadness Grace was already feeling. Grace and her ma hadn't had many conversations on the subject; there hadn't been much chance before Ma was gone. But Ma had told Grace enough to know that the right sort of man would only want to marry a girl who was a virgin. Grace smiled ruefully at the memory of that innocent conversation from what now seemed a lifetime ago.

"Ma, there's no way I can be perfect as the Virgin Mary, so there's no hope of my ever getting married."

Ma had laughed. "No, no. I'm not talking about the *Mary* part. I'm talking about the *virgin* part."

Grace had been confused. Her young mind had always thought of 'Virgin Mary' as being pretty much one long word, *virginmary*, sort of like the way her da would say *jesusmaryandjoseph*.

"Sweet child. Virgin means you haven't yet been with a

man."

"Well, then, I'm not a virgin, either. Sometimes I walk to and from school with one of the boys."

Running a loving hand through Grace's long hair, Ma had said, "Dear girl, being with a man means when you're trying to have a baby together, or practicing for it, anyway. Most often it happens in a bed, but it doesn't have to."

"Ohhh ... ," Grace had replied. And that's where mother and daughter had left the conversation, both them probably thinking there would be plenty of time to pick it up again.

Grace's fragile smile faded completely when she recalled her experience now of being "with a man." How she wished she was still a virgin, waiting for someone to love her. How she wished she could have been with a man in a bed instead of against that rough granite wall behind the library. She wanted to cry, again, still.

But she steadied herself instead. There being nothing else she could do, Grace washed the caked blood off her face, the blood she'd not had the energy to clean off, or even look at, the afternoon before. Then, she brushed her matted hair before pulling it back and weaving it into a loose braid down her back. She looked at the pile of rumbled clothes next to her bed. They were soiled and torn, much as she was now. She wanted to toss them in the burn barrel out back of Murphy's and watch them turn to ash. But that was a luxury Grace could ill afford. She didn't have many clothes, or the money for more, so she knew she would eventually mend them the best she could and scrub them as clean as the lye soap would get them. As for herself, Grace had no hope her body would mend properly or that any amount of scrubbing would make her clean again.

"Don't think about it. Don't think about it. Don't think about it," Grace kept repeating to herself as she concentrated on simply putting one foot in front of the other while descending the stairs to help Murph get breakfast ready for the early birds.

Weeks after Jack had met up with Grace, she still wouldn't have anything to do with him, and it was making him mad—really mad. And that pest, Tommy Miller, was walking her to and from the streetcar more now than ever. Her *escort*.

Jack had tried talking to Grace, but she just walked past as if he wasn't even there. As far as Jack was concerned, she'd had plenty of time to get over any misunderstanding they might have had. He knew what women were like. They all wanted the same thing. They wanted what Jack had given Grace. But now, the girl wouldn't even look in his direction. Jack didn't like being ignored. He wasn't much good at controlling his temper, either.

Growing up on the gritty streets of London, Jack had

been kicked out of the filthy room he'd shared with his ma more times than he could count when one strange man after another came through the door and his ma hollered for him to get out and don't come back 'til morning because she was gonna be workin' all night.

Well, Grace might not talk to him, and her little Tommy Miller might like to think he was her knight in shining armor, but Tommy was just a kid. Jack had known Tommy's ma for a long time, and he decided to pay her a visit.

The next morning, Jack caught up with Mary while she was on her way to work. It was a little early. Jack wasn't used to being up so soon after sunrise, but he wanted to get this out of the way.

"Wait up, Mary."

"I'll not. What do you want, Jack?"

"Aw, now Mary, I'm hurt. Is that any way to talk to an old friend?" Jack asked as he took off his woolen flat cap and crossed it over his heart.

"You've never been my friend, old or otherwise. So, again, what do you want? And hurry up with it because I need to get to work."

"Well, Mary, if I'm not your old friend now, I'm about to become him. You see, Tommy has taken to being bodyguard to that Grace who works for Murph, and he's bein' much too good at it."

"Ah, now it's Grace that you're wantin'. I heard you've

already had her."

Jack dropped the charm. "Shut up, Mary. Whatever I've had or not of Grace, it's none of your damned business. But Tommy *is* your business. And I'm thinking you probably want to keep him safe."

Stopping suddenly, Mary turned toward Jack and put her hands on her ample hips. "You don't scare me, Jack Barrett. Just tell me what the bloody hell you want."

Jack could feel his temper starting to boil over. "All right, Mary. I want you to call off your sonofabitch son. Tell Tommy to stay the hell away from Grace."

"Why? So you can have your way with her again? Tell me, if you can, why I would do that."

"Well, Mary, maybe it don't have anything to do with Grace. Maybe it's so Tommy don't end up dead like his da."

"What're you talkin' about? You know nothin' about Tommy's da."

"I know Tommy don't have a da. And I'm just sayin' I think you don't want to be referring to your son as 'poor dead Tommy' anytime soon, like they talk about his poor dead da. And you can see that don't happen."

"What're you sayin', Jack?"

"I'm *sayin'*, Mary, you want Tommy's heart to keep beatin', you keep him away from Grace."

Jack turned to head back in the direction he'd come from, but not before catching the faint smile that crossed

Mary's face. It sent a momentary chill down Jack's spine. But once he was alone again, Jack was soon feeling pretty good about how he'd finally taken care of the Tommy problem. And, thinking about the various ways he would have Grace again, he started whistling a cheerful tune from back home and strutting down the street like a Bantam rooster.

Jack should have paid closer attention to Mary's smile.

Like so many others, Mary's family had come from Ireland wanting nothing more than to find something to eat. When the blight attacked the potatoes, and the British shipped Ireland's other, healthy crops out of the country, leaving Mary's people to starve, America became their beacon of hope. It left Mary with no love for the British, especially the likes of Jack Barrett. After leaving their desperate lives in Ireland, Mary's family made its way across its new homeland, while enduring many of the Indian Wars, the Mexican American War, and, ultimately, the Civil War. Settling in Washington was as far from the country's inner struggles as it was possible to get. Mary had come from tough stock. Jack Barrett was no challenge to her.

And Mary knew about Jack and his kind. They were the ones full of self-importance. They had come from nothing and got by on their wit and their charm. But the fact was, they were shells on the outside, empty on the inside, and they wasted the life the good Lord gave them. Jack thought he was so smart, but he was nothing but a bully. And as for Tommy's da? While Jack was running his mouth, Mary had soon realized Jack knew nothing about him or his demise. Tommy's da hadn't been a great man and, sure, he'd liked his drink as much as Jack did, but that was all he and Jack had in common.

Enough was enough. Mary knew she should have taken care of the problem that was Jack Barrett before he'd done what he had to Grace, and she was truly sorry about that. But the threat to her Tommy? That was the last straw.

CHAPTER 7

September 30, 1908

Dear Eldri,

Gus and I have been spending a lot of time at the fishing shack. The catch has been good this year. But pretty soon, the days will be too cold and it will be dark too early for much fishing, and I'll have to stop until spring comes around again. Sometimes Alf joins us, but mostly he is happy just to be with Anna. At the end of the day, though, I usually take my catch to Anna, and she fries up a real good dinner for the three of us.

Maybe one day something I say to you in a letter will make you decide to come back to Conway and give me a second chance, or to at least write me back. That is my hope, anyway.

Your loving husband,

Ole

As the days passed, one after another, Eldri was surprised to find herself thinking more and more about Ole. She'd been so mad in the beginning that she couldn't get past his deception. But time often takes the edge off anger, and Eldri started looking beyond the deception and remembering the way Ole smiled, how kind he was to Gus, his steadfast friendship with Alf, his sincerity and, yes, even his clumsy attempts at thoughtfulness. Could what happened at the courthouse have been yet another clumsy attempt—at what? Had she failed to see an innocence behind his deception? No, Eldri wasn't ready to go that far. She wasn't ready to let Ole off that easily.

In the meantime, Eldri had found a way to make herself useful at Marta's house. Unlike her sister, Eldri enjoyed the calm rhythm of sewing. And she'd had to look no further than the ladies, and sometimes the gentlemen, living at Holm House to keep her busy. There was a constant stream of buttons or beads needing reattaching, seams being taken in or let out, and even whole dresses to alter or restyle.

The longer Eldri was at Marta's, the more often she heard a cry from the second floor, "Eldri, help me! I need to wear this dress tonight and just look at it. It's falling apart everywhere!" Of course, the cries usually came from Cissy, and Eldri always managed to repair the latest dress disaster, much to Cissy's delight and Albert's subsequent pleasure.

For her part, Marta couldn't have been more pleased, or
relieved. She hated sewing as much as Eldri loved it. And
she was as bad at it as Eldri was good. Although Marta
wasn't usually one to indulge in nostalgia, she couldn't help
noticing how much Eldri reminded her of their mother as
she sat by the light, eyes close to the fabric, patiently
drawing her needle and thread in and out, sewing stitches
so delicate they were nearly invisible.

But sewing wasn't the only thing keeping Eldri busy.
She was determined to learn English, once and for all. Never
again would she let herself be fooled because of her own
ignorance.

As soon as she had the chance, Eldri enrolled in the
nearest elementary school, where she was assigned to the
sixth-grade class. It was humiliating to be placed among
children so many years younger than she, but the
humiliation of not being able to read, write, or speak
English was immeasurably worse. She wondered what the
teacher, Miss Levenger, would think of her attending school,
but she soon learned Miss Levenger was accustomed to
having one or two immigrants, who spoke little or no
English, in her class every term. And she was very good at
putting those special students at ease.

"Class, meet Eldri Holm. She's from Norway and has
joined us in order to learn English. I know you'll make her
welcome. And you are to leave your teasing and snickering

at the door. I'm talking to you, Bobby Nelson," Miss
Levenger had said as she glared at the boy with the
mischievous smile who was sitting in the second row at the
desk closest to the window. Miss Levenger had introduced
Bobby Nelson last term in much the same way that she was
now introducing Eldri, when he was newly arrived from
Sweden, and she could tell Bobby meant no harm; he was
just glad not to be the most recent immigrant in the class
anymore.

Eldri let out a sigh of relief, louder than she'd intended,
which made the children laugh and Miss Levenger scowl
back at them, but only briefly. She had been teaching long
enough to know when a laugh was meant as a good-natured
giggle or a cruel taunt.

After the first school day passed without major
embarrassment, Eldri found herself looking forward to the
mornings spent with Miss Levenger and the other students.
Neither Marta nor Eldri had had much opportunity for
schooling in Norway, and they both felt disadvantaged from
their lack of education. While Marta did well learning as she
went along, Eldri seemed better off in the structure of a
classroom. But as much as she would have liked to, Eldri
couldn't spend all day at the school. There was simply too
much to do at Marta's, so she stayed through the mornings
and left with the afternoons' assignments. Once the day's
mending was done, though, and things quieted in the house,

Eldri would pull the assignments out of her school bag.

Unlike Eldri, Marta had realized early on that she needed to learn English. She didn't want anything to limit her choices. From the time they had boarded the ship that would take them to America, Marta was listening and learning. Eldri might have thought Marta was simply flirting as she strolled the ship's promenade with each different escort, and maybe there was a little of that. But Marta had also used every escort as an opportunity to practice her English. Those strolls might have been quite pleasant—but they were valuable English lessons as well.

Later, as the train trip that took the sisters from New York to Washington state had progressed, Marta's English had progressed as well. Eldri had admired Marta's efforts, but, for her, every new day had been full of new sights and sounds. She couldn't be bothered to put her nose in a book, she didn't read well anyway, and she was too shy to engage a stranger in conversation. So she had deferred to Marta and let her do the talking for both of them.

Ole and Alf were spending their Saturday morning at Ole's fishing shack on the Skagit. The day was cool and drizzly, but they figured unless it started dumping rain, they'd stay put. Gus was with them, and so far her digestive system was cooperating. Thank God for small favors.

"Anna wants a house," Alf said.

"No surprise there. The surprise is that Anna waited so long to tell you. That honeymoon castle you built does leave something to be desired."

"Hey, wait just a damned minute. As I recall, it was you who helped me build it. So if Anna is unhappy with it, you share some blame."

"You could look at it that way. But I accept no blame for however substandard the castle you brought Anna home to."

"Yup, that's how I'm gonna look at it. Anyway, I guess I should count myself lucky Anna stayed with me at all, after seeing the place."

"Anything is better than living under Mrs. Brotvik's roof."

"That's not a very high bar to clear. I tell you, when we went to collect her things, Anna wasted no time packing up. If she could have sneaked in and out the door without seeing the old lady, she would have been just as glad. But no, Mrs. Brotvik was waiting for us and kept muttering about losing such a good worker, which she'd never said while Anna worked there, until we were out of earshot. Not only that, she gave Anna an earful about Eldri leaving, too. God, what a miserable creature. But never mind that. I have an idea, Ole, and it involves you."

"How so?" Ole's expression showed his skepticism.

"Well, I'm thinking it's time we left that logging camp.

We should take that land we bought a couple years ago and do something with it."

"Ya, sure, we could grow daffodils or tulips." Ole said aloud to Alf. And to himself, "Or lilacs."

"You're not serious?"

"Nope."

"Well, that's a relief. I know some folks are trying out the idea of growing flowers, but, personally, I can't imagine anyone would want daffodils or tulips over corn, peas, green beans, or squash. They want pork and beef, too. And they want milk. But flowers? Nah. I'll leave the flowers to Anna. She can plant all she wants in the yard, around the house, wherever."

"Enough about the flowers, Alf. Tell me the rest of your big idea."

"You move out of the logging camp, live in the honeymoon castle with Anna and me while we build a house, maybe two, and start up farming together. We've worked hard these past years at the camp and made some money— but it was all for someone else. It's time we worked hard for ourselves."

"I'll just bet Anna can't wait to have another body underfoot in that little place. And then there's Gus, and what she contributes to the air in a room, always at the worst possible times."

"Anna wouldn't mind, I'm sure. She likes you, and she

would get used to Gus."

"Wait a minute. You haven't told her? Jesus, if you aren't about the dumbest husband."

"*You're* calling *me* the dumbest husband?"

"Second dumbest," Ole said, flinging a small, flat rock across the surface of the river.

"Five skips. That's pretty good," said Alf. "Anyway, I'm sure it would be okay with Anna."

"Anna is a good sport, Alf. But all of us in that tiny cabin? No, that's too much to expect of her, or anyone, for that matter. And, dumb husband that I am, I've had a lot of time to think about expectations. You're right, though, I'm ready to be done with logging and living in the camp. And maybe the cooks do their best, but the food is always tasteless and never hot. I tell you what, I'll quit the camp, but I will not move into your little cabin. There's plenty of space in the barn. I can put up a couple of walls and make a separate room—away from the other animals." Ole laughed. "In the meantime, if Anna will still feed me a hot meal once in a while, I sure won't turn her down."

"The barn? I'm not gonna let you live in the barn, and I know Anna won't."

"Then I'll have to say no to your offer, because I'll not impose on Anna any more than a hot meal. Besides, maybe it doesn't have to be for long. How about this? As soon as we have some walls up on your new house, enough so you and

Anna can move in there, I'll take over the castle."

"I don't know."

"Well, that's the deal. Take it or leave it."

"Okay. But I bet Anna will have something to say about it."

"Maybe. You got any tobacco?"

Alf pulled out his pouch and rolling papers. After lighting up, the men went back to concentrating on catching the river trout Anna would fry for dinner that night.

During the quiet, Ole got to thinking about the logging camp he'd called home for the past few years. It hadn't been all bad. Alf was right: He'd saved a little money, bought the land next to Alf on Fir Island, and bought this spot next to the Skagit, where he'd put up the fishing shack. And he'd met men from all over the world and learned that, regardless of where they'd come from, folks were pretty much the same on the inside. There were good ones and bad; honest ones and dishonest; smart and, well, maybe not so much; hardworking and lazy. He'd learned they all had more in common than not. But he was more than ready to be done living with them. He was ready to do something useful with the logs he, Alf, and the others in the camp had worked so hard to cut.

When it started getting dark, they packed their gear and the day's catch, loaded them up in Ole's wagon and drove to the barge that would carry them across to Fir Island.

"Ho, ho, Anna. We're here, and with some pretty good fish," Alf called as he unlatched the door of the cabin.

"And are those fish cleaned and ready for the frying pan yet?"

"They will be soon."

Ole left Alf to do the cleaning while he pulled the wagon into the barn. As he unhitched the horses, he took a good look around and saw where he could put up a couple of walls. Alf was right: He was ready to build a house. And no small part of that was the abiding hope that maybe, one day, Eldri would come back to live in it with him.

Once the horses had been tended to and the fish cleaned and fried, the three friends sat down to dinner.

"Good news, Anna. Ole is gonna help me build your house. He's moving into the barn, if it's okay with you."

"It is most definitely *not* okay with me. I'll not let you live in a barn, Ole Larsen."

Alf smirked and gave his friend a "told you so" look.

"Listen Anna, if anyone deserves her own house, it's you for putting up with this husband of yours," Ole replied. "I'm happy to help and, as I told Alf, I'm hoping I can keep getting a hot meal from you once in a while. But I'll not accept any more than that."

Anna was more stubborn than her husband, but in the end she, too, relented. However, she went on to win the second round by insisting Ole get every hot meal from her, not just the occasional one. "I'm thinking you won't need them for too long, though. I wouldn't be surprised if Eldri soon figures out what she's left behind and comes back to her home, and to you."

"Thank you, Anna. One can only hope."

The rest of the evening was filled with animated conversation and lots of ideas about Anna's house, some of them good and written down, others not so good and soon forgotten. Later that night, when Ole finally left to go back to the camp, he realized he was smiling. Perhaps he was beginning to hold out a little of that hope.

November 2, 1908

Dear Eldri,

Alf has decided to build a farmhouse. Anna has had enough of the little cabin he built just before they got married, and she's tired of being alone there during the day while he's over at the logging camp. As you know, the cabin is pretty rough. It's cold and drafty, too. But Anna doesn't complain, well, not too much, and has made the best out of living there.

Not long after Alf and I started working at the

camp, we pretty much figured out logging wasn't the work we wanted to do forever. So we bought that land on Fir Island where Alf built the cabin. He's going to quit the camp and build Anna's house. I'll be helping him. Anna is quite excited. Quite excited. (I said that twice to remind you just how excited Anna can get.)

I've never seen another couple so happy together. I had expected we would be as happy as they are. I don't expect that anymore, but I do hope for it.

In the meantime, maybe one day you will write me back.

Your loving husband,

Ole

CHAPTER 8

Marta found Eldri sitting in the parlor near the big front window that let in the afternoon light, a pile of mending folded in the large basket on the floor next to her.

"What are you working on now, Elle?"

"Cissy has torn another hem."

"That's no surprise, although how she manages to do it so often certainly is." Marta paused a moment. "I've had a letter from Jan," said Marta.

"Oh?"

"It seems our brother has gotten himself into some trouble with the farm, rather serious trouble. Here, you need to read this for yourself." Marta handed Eldri the letter.

Eldri put down her mending and adjusted her new glasses and thought about the day she'd put them on for the first time. It was as though a whole new world had opened up to her. She had no idea she'd not been seeing the world the way everyone else saw it.

For as long as she could remember, Eldri's world had seemed covered with a gauze film. But with her new glasses, gone were the headaches that had so often plagued her at the end of the day. She began to enjoy reading for the first time, and threading the eye of a sewing needle? A challenge no longer.

Thus the reason that, as Eldri looked at her brother's familiar handwriting, she blessed Miss Levenger, something she did often, for being the one to figure out that the reason Eldri couldn't read well was because she couldn't see well.

October 6, 1908

Dear Marta,

I hope you are fine. Things here at home are not so good.

We have had a hard year. Although our crops have done well, prices for wheat and potatoes are down.

Dagmar insists I get rid of the field workers, and it's true we will have more for ourselves if I to do that, but where would those people go? Farming is the only thing they know how to do. And I don't think Dagmar realizes how much harder we will have to work if I do let them go.

We've not used good judgment, and we've

expanded too fast. When Dagmar's uncle wanted out, we bought his farm. Then, to keep up, we bought one of those new threshing machines. It's good to have more land and some mechanization, but I had to borrow heavily in order to do it. Also, Dagmar and I haven't been as thrifty as we could have been. We've missed some payments, so the bank has told us we need to catch up or they will call our loan. Without a loan, we cannot pay our creditors or workers, and we will lose the farm.

I do not know your circumstances, but if there's any amount you might be able to send to help get us through this hard spot, I would be forever grateful.

I realize you have no love for Dagmar, and you might not want to help me, especially because it will also help her. Since you and Eldri left, I've seen Dagmar for who she really is. I'm sorry I didn't see it sooner. If I had, maybe you wouldn't have had to leave.

I didn't expect to miss you and Eldri as much as I do. But I ask that you not judge Dagmar too harshly. For her whole life, she was treated as though she didn't matter. All she had was her beauty and her pride. Now that her beauty is fading, her pride is softening as well. She is a good mother to our boy, and she keeps a clean house. If I don't have a perfect marriage, well, I have no one to blame but myself. All of you, including Far and Mor, tried to warn me away from Dagmar, but I was flattered by her attentions and deaf to your warnings. However poor my judgment, I am living the life of my own making.

If you are able, I hope you will help us. Either way, please send an answer as soon as possible.

Love to you and Eldri,

Your brother Jan

"Dear God. Marta, we have no choice. We have to help him." Eldri took off her glasses and pinched the bridge of her nose as though that would relieve the stress caused by reading her brother's unhappy letter.

"I know, Elle. And we will. Just let me be mad at Jan for a moment longer and let me say, I knew this was coming."

"We both knew."

Marta took in a deep breath. "Here's what I'm going to do, and soon, because Jan's letter is already over a month old. I'll send the money to pay off the bank loan, but Jan will have to sign ownership of the farm over to me."

"You would do that? Can you do it? Will Jan agree? I mean, do you think he would really sign the farm over to you?"

"Uff da! So many questions at once. Yes, I have the means to buy the farm. John and I have done quite well here. And Jan? He has no choice. Either I own the farm, or he loses it to the bank, and then Jan, Dagmar, and their little one will be homeless."

"I want to help."

While tucking the lock of loose hair back behind her sister's ear, Marta said, "Sweet Elle, there is nothing you can do. We both know money is the only thing that will help Jan right now. Besides, you know how much I have always wanted to be a farmer!"

"Ya, sure. Marta Holm, farmer. I could never, ever have imagined. But, thank you. I do not know what I would do if we did not have the farm anymore."

"I know, Elle. As much as I wanted to leave it, the farm is still our home."

When Marta had left the room, Eldri looked out the window and thought about life back in Rissa.

Eldri and Marta hadn't grown up with many earthly
comforts. The farm wasn't much, but its fertile soil along the
Trondheim Fjord provided hay for the livestock and enough
potatoes and wheat to keep Eldri's family fed, with a little
left over to take to market. Everyone—Far, Mor, Jan, Marta,
and Eldri—worked the farm. Eldri couldn't remember a time
when she'd not had some kind of chore: collecting eggs from
the chicken coop, while trying to avoid the painful pecking
and incessant crowing of those awful roosters; milking the
cows; skimming cream; or churning butter. Luckily, she
usually got out of the worst chore, the one no one wanted to
help with. Jan often teased Eldri about her weak stomach,
but it was a small price to pay to avoid helping with
slaughtering and butchering, the chore that never failed to
make her lose the whole of the last meal she'd eaten.

In the evenings, after dinner, Mor, Marta, and Eldri had
wool to spin, socks to darn, and rag rugs to weave while Far
and Jan were outside doing the evening milking. But once
the last of the day's chores were done, the family would
often gather in front of the evening fire and listen to Far
read aloud from one of the precious few books in the house.

But Marta, ah, Marta. She was the one who kept the
family smiling—and her parents a little worried. Marta
always wanted a bigger life than she had on the farm. Marta
was the dreamer.

Jan was the one with the relaxed charm. Eldri looked up

to her strong and handsome brother, who was never at a loss for the affections of one or another of the girls in the village. Things began to change, though, when Jan met Dagmar. She was beautiful, and Jan was immediately smitten. Unfortunately, that beauty blinded him to Dagmar's hard and greedy heart, and it wasn't long before the couple was married. When Dagmar came to live in the house with Eldri's family, she seemed to suck all the joy out of any room she was in and replace it with a tension felt by everyone except, of course, Jan.

Mor and Far made the unpleasant situation bearable, but when they passed during that terrible winter of 1905, everything changed. Dagmar wanted Marta and Eldri gone, and until she got her way, Jan had no peace.

Marta and Eldri didn't give up easily. They tried to make Jan understand what was happening. "Don't you see? She wants to turn you into a sofa farmer. Is that what you want to be? The one who lounges around all day while others do the work? Mor and Far would be ashamed." But in the end, Marta and Eldri could see they were beaten. They loved their brother enough to leave him and the farm that was, in fact, all the life they knew.

When the tension became unbearable, the sisters finally relented. Yes, they would leave, but with no money of their own, Jan would have to pay for their travel—to America.

"America? You can't go to America!"

"Jan, you may be able to tell us to leave the farm, our family's farm, but you cannot tell us where we will go," Marta replied.

"I thought you could go to Trondheim or maybe Kristiania."

"So I could become someone's maid?" Marta spat.

"That is not all you could do, Marta. There is more than one missionary who would be glad to have you for a wife."

Marta couldn't hold back the laugh that threatened to choke her. "Me? A missionary's wife? Jan, if you think that even a possibility, I am sad to say you do not know me at all."

Jan finally agreed to the deal and somehow found the money to send his sisters to America. Of course, Dagmar complained about the cost, but she was glad to be ridding herself of Jan's sisters. "The sooner the better," was all she had to say. Jan hoped his own life would be calmer with his sisters gone, but he wasn't so sure.

Once they decided to leave, Marta and Eldri were as eager as their sister-in-law to make it happen as soon as possible. But arrangements had to be made and details attended to. First, and most important, they needed to stay healthy. They also needed passports and a sponsor in America. Their *Tante* Lena was the only person they knew in America. Far's brother and his wife had gone to America several years earlier. Their uncle had died, but his widow,

Aunt Lena, still lived in Brooklyn, which a few years earlier
had become part of New York City. If she didn't write back
or, worse, if she turned down her nieces' request, Marta and
Eldri didn't know what they would do. One thing was sure:
Marta would not stay in Norway to become a maid or a
missionary's wife.

While the sisters waited for the answer from America,
Dagmar made everyone's lives, especially Jan's, a living hell.
She refused to help with the chores and, more than once,
kicked over the freshly filled milk pails—accidentally, or so
she would claim. Her dinner, which she never helped cook,
was never right: it was too salty or not salty enough, too cold
or too hot. And if she wasn't complaining, she was holed up
in the bedroom she shared with Jan, the bedroom that had
once belonged to Mor and Far, refusing to come out for days
at a time. Marta and Eldri almost, but not quite, pitied their
brother the abuse he had to endure; and they could hardly
wait to be done with it all.

Tante Lena's reply finally arrived: She would be
delighted to sponsor the young women and looked forward to
welcoming them into her home.

Holding their aunt's letter in her hands and hugging her
sister, Marta said, "This is it, Elle. We are finally going to
America. I can tell you, there is not one day I will miss
digging for potatoes or milking a cow. And I will die happy if
I never have to eat another herring—pickled or otherwise."

With the sponsorship question resolved, the other requirements for emigration soon completed, and the steamship agent's documents signed off at the police station, Marta and Eldri packed their few belongings and, passports in hand, prepared to leave Rissa.

When that day finally arrived, Eldri awoke to her favorite smell: lilac. She wrapped her shawl around her shoulders and walked outside, into the cool morning.

"I am sorry to be leaving you behind. Far and Mor planted you when I was born, and look at you now. You have shaded me, and your fragrance has made my life sweeter. I will never grow as tall as you, but I hope I will grow as strong. Your sweet smell is my favorite, you know, and I am sure that for the rest of my life, the scent of lilac will remind me of home. Goodbye, dear friend."

The rest of the morning was dark and cold, much like everyone's mood. Jan used the farm's old wagon to drive his sisters into town and down to the dock where they would catch the ferry to Trondheim. The goodbye was a sad one, but not in the way of most goodbyes. No, this one was sad because of the chill that had grown between brother and sisters where once there had been such love and warmth.

In Trondheim, Marta and Eldri boarded the train bound for Kristiania, where their ship was docked and waiting for them. If not for the noise of the train and the rhythmic drone of the wheels turning along the tracks, the ride would have been silent. The sisters occasionally looked at each other but had nothing to say.

Of course, there was no one to see them off on that April day in 1906, when they boarded the Scandinavian Line steamship that would take them from Kristiania across the Atlantic to New York in America. But they didn't mind. Mor and Far were gone, and they had lost Jan as well. There was nothing left for them in Norway.

Marta and Eldri dragged their bags down the stairs and sank into the bunk of the third-class cabin, their living quarters as they moved from their old home to their new.

Suddenly, the ship's deafening horn blew, signaling its imminent departure from Norway's shores.

"Come. Now, Elle. Hurry!" Marta grabbed her sister's arm and yanked hard. "We need to get up on deck."

"Ouch, Marta. What are you doing?" Eldri asked, rubbing her bruised elbow.

"Over here." Marta shoved her sister against the starboard side guardrail facing the dock. "Let's have a little fun. See that family over there? They're waving at us. Goodbye, goodbye, we will miss you!" Marta said while waving her favorite white, lace-trimmed handkerchief.

"What are you doing?"

"I am waving goodbye to my family. Oh, look, over there! Goodbye, goodbye ..."

"Marta, have you gone crazy? You do not know those

people. Not those there or those other ones."

"I have not gone crazy, Elle. But if my real family is not going to see me off, then I will invent one that will. See over there? It is Mor and Far."

"Ya, now I see them," Eldri said as her gaze caught an older couple who looked to be waving directly at her and Marta, with tears in their eyes.

CHAPTER 9

The Atlantic crossing took less than two weeks, but for
Eldri, it seemed to last a lifetime—a long, miserable
lifetime. She was as sick during the crossing as she had ever
been the few times she'd had to help with the butchering on
the farm. Dying would have been a mercy.

Unaffected, herself, by the motion of the sea, Marta
spent much of her time wandering the promenade and the
various decks, rarely alone. But she faithfully brought what
little food she thought Eldri might keep down, mostly thin
chicken broth, soda crackers, and an endless stream of hot
tea, all the while trying to assure Eldri her nausea would
eventually pass. It never did, and Eldri kept herself
quarantined below for as much of the crossing as possible.
But when their ship finally arrived in New York harbor,
Marta rushed below to drag a protesting Eldri out of her
bunk.

"Oh Marta, please just leave me. I am quite sure I will
be sick if I go above."

"Elle, I will not let you miss this sight."

"I am filthy, and I smell awful. It will be humiliating."

"No, you are coming with me. Do not bother to change
your dress. Just put on your travel coat. I will straighten

your hair. We are all rumpled and smelly from this long journey. No one is going to notice how you look."

"Are you sure?"

"I am."

"Well, all right. But I need help to get up."

"I will always help you, Elle."

As soon as they arrived above deck and leaned, for the second time, against the ship's guardrail, which was already crowded with their fellow passengers, they saw her: the Statue of Liberty. Suddenly, all went quiet. And the only movements were those of the ship, as it steamed into the harbor, and the tears that fell unchecked from the passengers' eyes. Spontaneously, some of the passengers started reciting Emma Lazarus's words engraved on the plaque at the statue's base:

> *Give me your tired, your poor,*
> *Your huddled masses yearning to breathe free,*
> *The wretched refuse of your teeming shore.*
> *Send these, the homeless, tempest-tost to me,*
> *I lift my lamp beside the golden door!*

The spell of Lady Liberty was quickly broken, however, by the reality of Ellis Island. The third-class passengers were soon lined up to board the transport ferry that would shuttle them from their ship through the immigration station doors on that small island in Upper New York Bay where they would join all manner of people, speaking a babel of languages and sharing the weariness of their travels. They also shared a dread of the medical examination, especially the one for trachoma. Everyone knew a diagnosis of trachoma nearly always meant rejection and a return home, unescorted if you were older than twelve. During their crossing, Marta and Eldri heard every awful story about the medical examination. They had tried to balance the naysayers' stories with the optimists' assurances that very few immigrants, especially those from Norway, were turned away because of the examination. But, still, they worried.

When their own turn came around, it was difficult for the sisters to contain their fears as they watched the sad faces of the weary immigrants who were singled out and rejected. They also couldn't help noticing that only their fellow passengers from third class were subjected to the humiliations of Ellis Island. A ticket in first or second class was also a pass directly into New York.

"Next!" Marta grabbed Eldri's hand and rushed toward the uniformed guard signaling them, only to find themselves waiting in yet another line.

"*Skit.*"

"Marta!"

"I am sorry, Eldri, but we will not accept being treated this way. We got all the right paperwork, we paid for our passage, and now we go from line to line in pens like herded cattle? Shit, I say."

"Please try to stay patient. It is no worse for us than for anyone else," Eldri said, looking with wonder at the mass of humanity surrounding her. "Look over there, Marta. What is that man doing?"

"Skit, where is my buttonhook?"

"Marta!"

"Elle, do you not see what he is doing? I will not let him grab my eyelid, or yours, with the filthy buttonhook he's using on everyone else. Look where he's wiping it off in between eye checks. His white coat is disgusting. If I must do this, it is going to be with my own instrument and not his."

When her turn arrived, Marta handed over her buttonhook. "Use this, please. On me and my sister, who is next after me. And do not wipe it on your coat."

A puzzled look crossed the face of the "eye man," and he shook his head. But in the end, he took the buttonhook from Marta's hand and used it to curl her right eyelid inside out. The pain was as excruciating as anything Marta had ever experienced, and she could barely keep from crying out. Instead, when the exam was over, she looked back at Eldri and nodded for her to come forward.

The efficiency of Ellis Island's processing operation was remarkable. In only a few hours, the inspectors and doctors, with the help of interpreters, some of whom spoke up to fifteen different languages, had screened and examined Marta and Eldri, and the thousands of other immigrants who passed through Ellis Island that day. The sisters pinned their landing cards to their blouses, Marta put her buttonhook back in her bag and, after exchanging their Norwegian krone for U.S. dollars at the Money Exchange booth, they were ready to leave the immigrant warehouse behind and exit via the Stairs of Separation, which led toward the ferry that would shuttle them to New York City's Brooklyn neighborhood.

"Uff da. Marta, not another boat," moaned Eldri. She could already feel the bile gathering in her throat.

"Come on, Eldri. It is just a short trip across the water. You've survived much worse, and this is the last one."

"Promise?"

"I promise. After this, no more boats."

"I hope you are right." Stepping onto the swaying vessel, Eldri took one last look at Lady Liberty.

During the harbor crossing, Eldri managed to keep the nausea of her motion sickness under control, but just when she thought she was safe, the stench coming from the nearby Gowanus Canal nearly knocked her over.

"Marta! The smell. How can anyone bear it?"

"It is truly awful. Cover your nose with your handkerchief. Maybe it will help."

Eldri did as Marta suggested, picked up her bag, and debarked the boat. On the wharf, she and Marta were hailed by Leif, the father of a young family they had met aboard during their ocean crossing. "*Kommer pa*! Come on, we are on our way to Lapskaus Boulevard, too. We will share our ride with you."

"*Lapskaus?*" asked Marta.

"Ya, that is what they call it, 'Stew Boulevard.'"

"Why lapskaus ... uh, stew?"

"I suppose because that's the part of Brooklyn where all the Norwegians live. Kind of a Norwegian stew of people, maybe. Come on now, first give me your bags then let me help you up."

While Leif and his wife held tightly to their two small children, the hired driver turned his jostling wagon this way and that. Nothing could have prepared this newest group of immigrants for the sights, smells, and sounds that enveloped them as they passed through the city. The press of people was everywhere, first on the sidewalks, then, suddenly and dangerously, dashing out into the street. The piercing stench of horse dung, which dropped so fast that the street sweepers couldn't possibly keep up, was gagging. The biggest surprise, however, came prefaced with a sudden, deafening roar.

"Marta, look. There is a train over our heads. How is that possible?"

"I cannot tell you, Elle. But it is a wonder," Marta screamed over the noise.

"Ish, look at this!" Elle said as she tried to brush the black grit that showered them while the El passed above. "My shirtwaist is ruined. What will Tante Lena think?"

"If anyone knows what it is like to pass under, over, and across these filthy streets, it is Tante Lena. Do not give it any more thought," replied Marta.

The wagon eventually stopped in front of a tidy brick row house. "Here we go, *damer*, the address on your letter. You ladies are at your new home. Let me help you down," said Leif.

"*Tusen takk*," said Eldri. A thousand thanks.

"*Lykke til!*" Leif shouted and waved while the driver spurred his horses on their way.

"And I hope you have good luck, too," Marta whispered. The exhausted travelers picked up their bags and climbed the steps of the narrow brownstone, checked the name and number on the door, and rang the bell. After their long journey, Marta and Eldri couldn't have been happier for the familiar smells of home seeping from under the front door. A rustle and scrape, a lock unlatched, and the heavy door opened. The woman who opened it was a little rounder, and much grayer, but she was surely their Tante Lena.

"Oh, my dears, my dears. *Velkommen*, welcome, to America! How good to see family again. Come, come, inside."

After the loss of their parents and the treatment by Jan and Dagmar, Marta and Eldri could not have been more grateful for the warmth of their aunt's welcome.

The dinner Tante Lena had waiting for them was simple but delicious.

"Thank you for dinner." Eldri, who had eaten almost nothing during the ocean crossing, was especially enjoying her meal. "It reminds me of the dinners our family shared when Mor and Far were still alive."

"I was sorry to learn the news of their loss. I am sure it was very difficult for you. And yet, you have a new sister. What is her name again?"

"Dagmar," Marta replied. "She is not our sister. She is our brother's wife."

"It is not good?"

"It is not. She is much of the reason Eldri and I had to leave Norway. She stole Jan's heart, and the rest of him as well. There was no room left for us at the farm."

"How sad. I suspect your brother, at least, will come to regret turning his back on you."

"Perhaps, but in the meantime, Eldri and I had to leave."

"Well, America is a wonderful place, and I expect you will be happy here. May I pass you the pickled herring?"

"Oh no, no, no!" exclaimed Marta while Eldri looked at her and smiled. "But I would enjoy a little more of the lapskaus."

Although it had been many, many years, Tante Lena
remembered the weariness of her own first night in
America, and she soon led the girls to the room that would
be their new home, at least for a while. They tried
unpacking some of their things, but didn't get far before
collapsing onto the double bed they were to share. The room
was more spacious, and the bed much bigger, than anything
they had ever had.

"I think I might get lost in here," said a weary Eldri.

Marta changed the subject. "America is where I have
always belonged. I am home."

"How can you possibly know that after only a few
hours?"

"If we come to the place that feels right, Elle, the sense
of belonging can be immediate."

During the next several weeks, the sisters stayed busy,
and paid a little rent, by helping their aunt with some of the
mending work that she took in. But then came the day
Marta threw down the piece she'd been working on and
exclaimed, "If I have to sew on another damned button, I
swear I will go mad."

"I think I could stay in New York, though. Tante Lena
says the shirtwaist factories are always hiring," said Eldri,
looking up from her own piece. "Maybe we could go there?"

"I can tell you I will not be taking on any sewing job,
that is for sure," said Marta.

"Would you just think about it? You do not like sewing, I know, but it would be steady work, and you might like it better than this piece work."

"Doubtful, but I will go with you."

Eldri's mind was certainly more open to the factory work than Marta's and, unlike Marta, she enjoyed sewing. But even her mind was changed the day she and Marta took the El, the elevated train that had so frightened them on the wagon ride from Ellis Island, over to the garment district in the Greenwich Village neighborhood of New York's Manhattan Island.

When Marta saw the awful buildings where the women inside were bent over sewing machines for hours and hours every day, she simply turned without a word or a backward glance and started walking back toward the El's landing. And although Eldri knew she could do the work, she, too, had hoped for more, for better, than this. Working day after day, year after year, on a crowded factory floor, windows blacked out with dirt and dust? Just the thought, and she could feel one of her headaches coming on.

"You were right, Marta," Eldri said on the ride back to Brooklyn. "My goals are not as great as yours, but I do admit that spending my days in one of those factories is not why I left Norway. Even I have hoped for better. But where shall we go? And how will we get there?"

"We will figure it out, that is all."

It was Tante Lena who came up with a solution. "First I must say that I will be very, very sorry to see you go. Your company has lightened my heart. But I am not surprised that you do not want to stay in New York, so I know I cannot talk you out of leaving. It is a good place to start a new life, perhaps, but it is not the right place for everyone.

"My sister, Gudrun, lives all the way across America in Washington state. She owns a boardinghouse in the town of Conway. It is a long way, even by train, but it is not nearly so crowded there as it is here. And maybe there are more, or better, opportunities for young women than what is left here in the city. I could write Gudrun a letter of introduction, and I am sure she will help you in any way that she can."

"You would do that for us?" asked Marta.

"Of course, I would. And if I were any younger, I would go with you."

On the day Marta and Eldri were to leave, while the cab waited to take them to the train station, tears pooled in Tante Lena's eyes as she handed her nieces the letter she'd written to her sister, along with a faded photograph. "This is so old, I am sure Gudrun no longer looks like the woman in the photo, but it is the only one I have. Promise me you will give her a hug and tell her how much I miss her."

CHAPTER 10

"Where to, miss?" asked the man behind the brass grill of the ticket booth.

"To Conway, in Washington," replied Marta.

"Well, *that's* gonna be a long trip. But we'll get ya' there. How do you want to travel? First class, second, or emigrant car?"

"Which is the lowest cost?"

"That would be the emigrant car. It's a very cheap way for newly arrived folks to travel on the railroads."

"That sounds good for my sister and me."

"You wouldn't say that if you saw those cars from the inside. I don't recommend you travel that way. But it's my job to offer it. Those emigrant cars are really just converted baggage cars. When the train is headed west, the railroad puts in some benches, a couple of water buckets, and a stove, crams as many people in there as they can, and then leaves them on their own. No food or blankets."

"Not so good."

"No, not so good at all. Some of the railroads are starting to offer tourist cars. They're a little better, but they're not available on this line."

"Two second class tickets, please."

"You got it."

"All aboard!"

"Hurry, Eldri. It's time."

"Coming." Eldri rushed toward her sister. While Marta had been in conversation with the ticket agent, Eldri had been preoccupied watching a well-dressed man, carrying a shiny black leather doctor's bag embossed with three gold initials at the clasp. He was also trying to enter the second-class car, but the conductor seemed to be arguing with him and refusing to let him board.

"My ticket says second class." The man was clearly confused and impatient.

"Don't care what your ticket says. Your people are in the car up front there," the conductor said.

"But as soon as we get going, that car will fill with smoke from the engine's stack. And I paid for second class!"

"Look, I don't make the rules, boy, but I do follow them. And the rules say you go in that car. Now, if you don't want to go to Chicago ..."

"I must go to Chicago. My family is there waiting for me."

"Then I suggest you get on board."

The black-skinned man conceded defeat, but not before

slapping his hat against his thigh in frustration.

"Don't you be doin' that, boy. I'll pull you right from this train."

"Sorry, sir."

"That's better. Now, get in that car."

"Yessir."

Eldri didn't need to understand English in order to understand what had just happened. "So many things that do not make sense," she muttered.

It took just a day, but certainly a very long day, for Marta and Eldri to travel from New York City to Chicago. After hours spent sitting on the stiff-backed, but slightly padded, train seat, they were glad for the convenience of a boardinghouse adjacent to the train station, where they spent a restless night. The room was sparsely furnished and noisy, but it was clean, and the bed was well-worn but comfortable enough.

Early the next morning, Marta and Eldri walked to the café at the train station and, not knowing when they might eat again, had themselves a filling breakfast of eggs, ham, toast with strawberry jam, and very strong coffee.

"Uff da, Marta, I think I will never need to eat again."

"You say that now, but in a few hours you will be glad of this breakfast. We should also find a place to buy some bread and cheese so we have something to eat on the train."

"Is that necessary? There are supposed to be many stops

along the way where we can get food."

"Ya, I know. But I will feel better if we take some with us."

They walked toward the bread stand, trying to ignore the smarmy smiles and leering eyes of too many gentlemen watching unaccompanied women making their way through the station.

"Have they no shame?"

"I do not think so, Elle."

"We are not *kvel*."

"No, *we* are not cattle. It is they who have no manners that are shameless kvel."

Suddenly, a nervous-looking young boy came rushing toward them. "Norsk?" he asked.

"Ya, we are Norwegian. Do you need something?" asked Marta.

"I do not speak English. I do not know where to go. I am supposed to get on the train to St. Paul, in Minnesota."

"Let me see your ticket." Marta held out her hand, and the boy complied. "Well, good. We are on the same train as you, but your ticket is for the emigrant car. Walk with us, and we will take you there."

"*Mange takk*, many thanks," said the boy, visibly relieved.

"You are welcome. My name is Marta, and this is my sister, Eldri. And you are?"

"I am Nels. Nels Olsen."

"Hello, Nels Olsen." Marta shook the boy's hand and, afterward, scowled slightly at the grimy residue on her palm. "How old are you?"

"I am seven *år gammel.*"

"Seven years old? Why are you traveling alone? You are too young," exclaimed Eldri.

"There is no one to travel with me. Mor and Far are gone. My aunt and uncle sent me this train ticket. I am going to live on their farm in Minnesota."

"Gone?" asked Eldri.

"Dead," replied the boy.

"Oh, Nels. I am so sorry," Eldri replied.

"I am sorry, too. I miss them lots. And when they died, some people came and got me and took me to the home."

"Home?" asked Eldri.

"Orphanage. It is not a good place, and I am glad to be leaving there."

"Come on, then. We will help you get to St. Paul and your aunt and uncle. But first, you need to go into the bathroom and wash your face and hands," said Marta. "We will be here when you come out."

"Promise?"

"Ya, we promise," said Eldri.

Nels seemed to lose an invisible burden that had been weighing him down. He did as he was told and walked into the bathroom, but when he emerged, he absentmindedly wiped his wet hands on the sides of his dirty trousers.

"Ish," Marta uttered under her breath. Eldri held a hand over her mouth to hide a smile.

The sisters led Nels to his train car. But when they looked inside, they quickly realized they could not leave him in the bedlam of the overcrowded emigrant car. The cacophony that came from shouting in so many different languages was deafening. And the acrid odor, a mixture of rotting food, unwashed bodies, and human waste, was nauseating.

Marta grabbed ahold of Nels's hand. "Come with us."

"Var?"

"I will tell you where. We are going to change your ticket. You will ride with us to St. Paul." Marta looked at Eldri, who simply nodded.

"But I have no money."

"We do not have much money ourselves, but we have enough for your ticket. And we will not let you ride in there." Marta said.

"I have been in worse."

"Maybe so. But not today," replied Eldri.

"Now I understand what the ticket man in New York meant when we asked him about the cheap fare of the emigrant car," Marta said to Eldri.

"Ya. He did us a favor when he told us to spend a little

more. I cannot say much good about second class, but it is surely better than what we just saw.

Once the three passengers were settled in their seats, Nels looked over at the cheese and bread that Marta had bought earlier that morning.

"And have you not eaten?" she asked.

"Not since last night. They took me to the train before breakfast time today."

Marta broke off a hunk of cheese and tore a piece of bread and gave it to Nels. She no sooner said, "Eat," than it was nearly gone.

"All aboard!" The last-minute passengers scrambled to board the train, which was soon on its way to St. Paul. Within minutes, Nels was slumped against Eldri and in a deep sleep.

"I am relieved we did not have to board that filthy car," Eldri whispered.

"I am, too, and glad we earned enough money to keep us from having to travel that way."

"I never thought I would hear you say you were glad for sewing work."

"I will always hate sewing, but if it keeps me out of one of those disgusting places, then I will do it."

"He is such an innocent. I hope we are taking him to a better life," Eldri said as she stroked the blonde hair of the sleeping child.

"I do too, Elle."

Nels slept soundly for several hours, then helped himself to another hunk of bread and cheese, which seemed to restore his energy and kindle his enthusiasm. As if in concert with the rhythm of the train's wheels rolling on the track, he kept repeating, "Look at that farm! Look at that farm!"

When the train arrived at the St. Paul, Nels glanced out the window at the station platform and began jumping up and down. "Over there! *Tante og oncle!*"

Marta and Eldri looked in the direction that Nels's small hand was pointing and were relieved to see a kindly looking, middle-aged couple—Nels's aunt and uncle. "I think we can leave Nels with them, Marta."

As soon as Nels jumped off the train step, he flew into the arms of his aunt and uncle.

"Nels! Here you are at last. And how much you have grown since the last time we saw you," said the woman, who hugged the boy, then looked up at Marta and Eldri as they approached, carrying the shabby travel bag that Nels, in his excitement, had left behind.

Looking up, Nels's aunt asked her nephew, "Who are these people?"

"Well, this is Marta, and this is Eldri. They are my new friends. I sat with them on the train from Chicago. They bought me a new ticket, and I had bread and cheese, too."

Marta stepped up to explain. "We are sisters recently from Norway. We are on our way from New York City to Washington state, and we met Nels in Chicago. We were going to put him on the emigrant car for his trip here, but ... well, have you ever been into one of those cars?"

"No, we have not. Was something wrong?" asked the man.

"It was not fit for *any* human, much less a child."

"Oh dear," said the woman. "We did not know. We just wanted to get Nels out of that orphanage and home with us. It was all we could afford."

"We understand, and we were happy to keep him safe on the train. Now it is up to you to keep him safe," Marta said.

"You do not need to worry about that. But, how can we thank you?" asked the man.

"Be good parents," replied Marta.

Eldri bent down and took hold of Nels's bony shoulders. "Goodbye, Nels. Behave yourself, now, and listen to your new far and mor."

"And wash your hands once in a while," Marta added.

The sisters hugged their temporary ward, then reboarded the Great Northern.

During the rest of their journey, past the plains of the Midwest states and across the Rocky Mountains, the sisters got almost no rest. Eldri was relieved she didn't suffer the motion sickness that had so plagued her on the Atlantic crossing, because every day brought new sights, smells, and sounds, and she didn't want to miss any of it. And as the train progressed, Marta's English progressed as well. There was no shortage of passengers, mostly eager young men, happy to engage Marta in conversation. But Eldri was too shy for that and had more trouble forgetting the lecherous looks they had gotten at the Chicago station than did her sister.

The late afternoon sun was sinking in the sky when, after a week spent sitting, watching, and waiting, the sisters' travels were finally at an end. They had arrived in Conway, where Tante Lena's sister lived.

Immersed in her own excitement in finally arriving at what would be her new home, Eldri didn't notice her sister had gone quiet. She took Marta's free arm into her own, "We are home. Truly, I feel we are finally home." Marta smiled, but she remained silent.

Approaching the first person they saw on the street, an older woman who seemed friendly enough, Marta showed her the photo Tante Lena had given them and asked if she knew Gudrun Brotvik. The brusque, almost harsh, reply from such a gentle-looking woman took both sisters by surprise.

"I don't recognize the woman in that photo, but I can tell you Brotvik's Boardinghouse is on the next street over. It's easy enough to find, and there's a sign over the door." The woman walked on, leaving Marta and Eldri to wonder what part of such a brief encounter could possibly have offended her.

Trying to forget the woman's tone and focus on her directions, the sisters finally saw a worn wooden sign hanging outside a plain, equally worn three-story building, "Brotvik's Boardinghouse." With more than a little apprehension, they walked up the creaky wooden steps. Their knock at the door was met with a frowning and formidable woman.

"Gudrun?" Marta asked.

"I am Mrs. Brotvik, ya. And you are?" came the reply.

"I am Marta Holm, and this is my sister, Eldri. Your own sister, Lena, is our aunt."

"My sister has no siblings but me. And I have no children. So, tell me, how is it you can be her nieces?" the woman said with a scowl.

"Tante Lena was married to our father's brother," replied Marta, biting her tongue to keep from saying something she would surely regret. "We have come from staying with her in New York. We have also brought you a letter, and we have instructions to give you a hug from her."

Arms outstretched, Eldri nearly fell over when Gudrun, or rather, Mrs. Brotvik, stepped back to avoid any attempt at physical contact.

"The letter, please."

Marta complied with the abrupt command. The sisters' confusion about the conversation with the woman in the street was satisfied. But they were surprised and upset to learn that this cold woman could actually be dear Tante Lena's sister. They waited while Mrs. Brotvik read the letter from her sister.

"Is there something else?" Mrs. Brotvik said.

"Well, we were hoping for a place to stay, at least for tonight," Marta replied.

"I have a small room, one bed. It is yours if you want it, and if you can pay for it."

"*Takk skal do ha.* You have our thanks. Ya, we can pay."

"Then come in. Hurry up! Do you not feel the draft?"

The sisters found themselves glad to be exhausted. It made the dried out and cheerless dinner Mrs. Brotvik provided seem less miserable, and as soon as they had finished eating, they went upstairs to the equally cheerless room Mrs. Brotvik had let to them.

"She looks nothing like her photo, Marta." The woman in the photo had bright eyes, an engaging smile, and a look of kindness about her.

"It is a lesson to us, Elle, to stay mindful that unhappiness inside can eventually turn a person ugly on the outside. Who knows what has happened to the woman in the years since that photo was taken?"

CHAPTER 11

Christmas Eve, 1908

God Jul, Eldri,

Merry Christmas, my dear.

It's cold and dark up here, and the days are short. But it is Christmas and time to celebrate the birth of our Lord.

Anna and Alf had me over for dinner tonight. Anna roasted a fat goose that Alf and I shot the other day. Of course, with Anna's cooking, it tasted delicious. And she served it with all the trimmings.

It was easy to find just the right tree for Alf and Anna's first Christmas together. After all the years Alf and I have spent logging, we know where to find the good ones. Anna liked decorating it with popcorn strands and dried apples and berries. I carved a star for the top and gave it to them. I think they liked it. Under the tree was a box with my name on it. Anna and Alf gave me a new felt bowler. They say I look quite smart in it. I'm not so sure about that, but I do like it.

Our simple Christmas in the country probably sounds pretty dull to you now that you've been in Seattle for a while. But simple as it was, or perhaps because it was simple, we enjoyed ourselves very much. We shared a prayer of thanksgiving and a prayer that you are well.

Your loving husband,

Ole

Jack Barrett left the bar at dusk. He pulled up his collar and tilted his hat against the rain that had started earlier in the day. He wasn't thinking about the weather, though. He was focused instead on the many ways he wanted to have Grace again, whether to bother trying to charm her or to just take her. But his thoughts should have been on the three men following him a few blocks behind. When Jack approached the library, he slowed and smiled at what he'd done there with Grace, giving the men their opportunity to catch up with him.

"Hey, Jack. We hear you had yourself some excitement here not too long ago."

"Huh? Oh, hey, fellas. What're you talking about?" Jack vaguely recognized the men from the Seamen's Home.

"You know, with that girl who works at Murphy's Bar."

"How do you know about her?"

As they surrounded Jack, one of the men said, "It's a mistake to make Miss Mary mad. She hasn't liked your bullying, but she was willing to overlook it. You made her mad enough with what you did to Grace. But when you threatened her Tommy, you made a grave mistake."

Jack knew he was in trouble, and he was scared. Hoping the men couldn't smell his fear, he tried blustering his way out of his predicament. "Why would Miss Mary care about some stupid girl? And she had to know I wasn't serious about Tommy."

"You're not helping yourself any, Jack. We all like little Grace."

"Well, gents, that makes four of us. I like 'little Grace,' too," Jack said with as much false bravado as he could muster. Too busy puffing out his chest and pulling down on his vest, Jack failed to guard against the first blow when it struck.

"Aw, God," Jack grunted, the wind knocked out of him. The punch to his gut doubled him over. The next one, the one to the back of his head, put him on the ground. All Jack could do was curl into a ball and hope it would soon be over. But as soon as the punches stopped, the kicking started.

Walking their beat early the next morning, Christmas day, the two cops found Jack's broken body lying in a heap against the same granite wall where he had taken Grace.

"Ain't he that troublemaker, Jack something?" said the one, as he roughly rolled the body onto its back with the muddy toe of his boot.

"Barrett. I think his last name's Barrett. Looks like he fell down those steps over there and crawled against this wall. It's been pretty rainy lately, and I'll bet those steps are slick," said the other.

"That's what I see, too. Probably slipped on the wet stone. It'd be a hard fall."

"Hard enough to kill a man, I'd say."

"Yup."

The coroner's wagon soon showed up. The cause of death was determined an accident, a drunken fall. Jack Barrett's remains were buried in the Duwamish Poor Farm Cemetery among all the others who had died with no one to claim them.

Marta's boardinghouse was full of Christmas cheer, with garlands of deep green and bright red berries adorning the hallways on every floor, a huge tree in the parlor, and every sort of delicious smell coming from inside Mary's kitchen. She was cooking enough food to feed an army. Certainly, it was more than the residents of Holm House could ever eat. But Marta had agreed to let Mary cook some extra, which Tommy would take to the Seaman's Home.

While decorating the Christmas tree, Eldri asked Marta how she came to buy such a fine house.

"Simple, Elle, I proposed to John," she said with a teasing smile.

"Marta!"

"Well, I didn't actually propose to him. I made him a proposal."

"And that was?"

"To buy this house together. Mrs. Halverson, who, you'll remember, owned the house when I moved in, had been thinking about selling for some time. Her children were grown and gone, and she was ready to quit working so hard.

"John and I were on an evening stroll along the water. The gray winter's day was cold and a little drizzly, but, of course, we're all used to the gray and damp. I was just glad for the chance to be together. I told John that Mrs. Halverson wanted to sell the boardinghouse, and I wanted to buy it. I didn't have the money, of course, but I was certain I could run the place; and I had an idea how to make it profitable, actually very profitable. As a typical boardinghouse, it would make out fine, but I thought there was a lot more money to be made by turning it into a place where couples like John and me could have a private and permanent residence."

Seeing the look of confusion on Eldri's face, Marta continued, "It's pretty simple, Elle. When this was Halverson's Boardinghouse, it provided me with a place to live. And that was fine. But what I saw was a better opportunity: offering an escape from real life to couples in circumstances similar to John's and mine. It's a business, though, not a charity, and escapes from real life don't come cheap."

Eldri looked less confused, but not by much. "Go on."

"After explaining my idea to John, I asked him to lend me the money to buy the house. He turned me down."

"He refused you?"

"He did, and in no uncertain terms. But as it turns out, he wanted to go in as equal partners. It was pretty clear I wasn't going to change John's mind, so I simply shook his hand and wished us luck.

"I admitted to John that my idea for the place was somewhat 'progressive.' You see, rather than keeping this a simple boardinghouse, or filling it with ladies who have no other means of earning a living and dirty men who are only too eager to pay for their services, I envisioned a place for people with genuine affection for each other—and the money—to be able to enjoy each other's company. John says in France, a place like this might be called a 'pied à terre,'" Marta said with a flourish of her right arm.

"Pied à terre ... I cannot even speak English yet, and you have already moved on to French. I am hopeless."

"Believe me, Elle, that is the only French I know." Marta laughed. "Anyway, the partnership established, my job was to redecorate, staff, and manage Holm House. In the meantime, John worked to find the occupants, which wasn't difficult. John is, by far, not the only man in Seattle who is married to the right sort of woman but in another kind of relationship with someone else. The folks who live here have a secure, discreet, and permanent place to call their own. They don't have to waste their precious time and energy looking for a place to meet. The men have the money to pay, and their ladies have a secure place to live. Except Susannah, of course, who has plenty of money of her own and no need for any more men in her life."

"What about the people who were already living here? What happened to them?"

"I admit that was a worry. I had to give them notice, of course, but I also gave everyone enough time to find other, equally satisfactory accommodations. And I'm glad to say they all left with no hard feelings."

"A relief, I am sure. We know what it is like to be put out of our home."

"We do, indeed. Anyway, as each boarder moved out, I furnished the empty room with soft colors on the walls, a warm rug on the floor, room-darkening drapes, a small dresser and mirror, a pair of easy chairs, a small dining table with two chairs, and, most important of all, a very comfortable double bed." Marta winked at Eldri. "I intentionally kept the furnishings spare and the colors neutral because I wanted the new residents to think of the rooms as their own and to accent them in whatever way would make them feel most at home.

"I covered the entryway, living, and dining rooms with these Oriental rugs. I also bought a few pieces of furniture from Sally Halverson, some of which are in your room. And, I bought her piano, which, given Tommy's talent, was certainly the best piece I acquired from her."

"Where did the glass hanging in the dining room come from? I do not believe I have ever seen anything like it. It is beautiful."

"Ah, yes. It is probably the finest thing in this house. It is certainly my most treasured. It is called a 'chandelier.'"

"Chandelier," repeated Eldri. "We surely did not grow up with anything so fine, Marta."

"We did not. It was a gift from John."

"A very nice gift."

"Isn't it, though? John had it shipped over from Murano, which is a small Italian island near the city of Venice and quite famous for its glasswork."

"I do see why," said Eldri as she watched the sunlight reflect off each rose-colored prism.

"There is one room that has gone untouched: the kitchen. Mary worked for Sally Halverson for several years and agreed to stay on after I purchased the house, but she made it very clear that it had taken her years to set up the kitchen just the way she liked it, and she wouldn't stand for anyone coming in and trying to change things."

"You made a wise decision, Marta."

"Ya, don't I know."

Ever since he'd seen Eldri, first at Brotvik's and then in the little white church, Ole had known he wanted to be with her, all the time. What he didn't know, however, was that Eldri was determined to have her own life before she shared it with anyone again. She'd never had anything she could call her own, In fact, one of her earliest memories was sharing a narrow wooden cot with Marta. And when they left Norway on the ship, they'd had that narrow bunk, the one Eldri was still ashamed to admit she was responsible for having made so putrid.

When the ship arrived in New York Harbor, though, and

Eldri saw that majestic statue holding the flame, all she could do was admire the strong, solitary woman welcoming the immigrants to America's shores. Eldri wanted the chance to be a strong, solitary woman, too. Not forever, perhaps, but at least for a while.

Had Ole known that, perhaps he'd not have made the fateful error in judgment at the courthouse in Mount Vernon. Ole's only experience with women was a mother who did her best, but he'd learned early on he couldn't rely on strengths she just didn't have. It might have been Eldri's strength that had first attracted him—and was working against him now.

Such was part of the problem, part of the reason Eldri had to get away. Ole didn't know her well enough to marry her. Although he'd asked about her home in Rissa and how she came to be in America, he'd not asked about who she was on the inside. He'd not understood that Eldri wanted to be with someone who asked her what she was thinking, and who would listen, really listen, to her answer.

CHAPTER 12

January 1, 1909

Dear Eldri,

*Happy New Year. May it bring us health,
happiness, and, hopefully, back together.*

I can think of nothing I would like better.

Your loving husband,

Ole

Oh, Ole, a lonely Eldri mused, I think your letters are
working. I do like Seattle, but I miss Conway more. And I
miss Anna and Alf. I miss Gus. And, yes, I especially miss
you.

Perhaps, Eldri thought, if she started writing Ole back,
she would learn whether or not he was a man who listened,
or could learn how to.

With the start of the new year, Eldri resolved to find out.

January 15, 1909

Dear Ole,

A Happy New Year to you.

You have worked so hard writing your thoughtful letters. Perhaps it is time I begin answering them.

That day at the courthouse, I figured you had decided you did not want to be alone anymore, that you were tired of doing your own laundry, cooking, and cleaning. I figured you wanted a wife, and almost any girl of marriageable age would do.

I have begun to think perhaps I did not realize your true feelings. That it was me, Eldri, you wanted to marry.

Sincerely,

Eldri

Short as the first letter was, it had taken a long time for
Eldri to figure out what she wanted to say and how to say it,
and she didn't finish it to her satisfaction until very late.
When she finally got into bed, exhausted from a full day of
schoolwork, mending, and the letter to Ole, Eldri expected to
fall right to sleep. But that's not how things go sometimes,
and this was one of those times. The questions, so many
questions: Could Ole really be a good man who had made a
dreadful mistake? Or was he merely an opportunist in the
guise of a good man? What might happen if I crack open the
door to my life and let him see inside? Is it possible for Ole
to fit into this new life I am building? Or will I just be fooled
again by him?

Eldri didn't fall sleep until the wee hours of the next
morning, when she had finally sorted out some of her
questions and answered as many as she could.

Grace dreaded the dawn of each new day. She knew her
dress, whichever one she chose, was going to fit tighter than
it had the day before, and her corset wouldn't hide her
condition forever.

What she didn't know was how she was going to get
herself out of the fix she was in. The bruises on the outside,
the ones on her skin, had healed up, and the limp was
hardly noticeable anymore. But the bruise Jack had left on

the inside kept growing and growing. She hadn't had her monthly since a week or two before he'd beaten and raped her.

Grace was doing her best, but all she had to look forward to when she got up in the morning was one more day of trying to keep going. She was grateful Murph had let her stay in the room after her parents died and for the work he gave her downstairs in the kitchen. But, little by little, the memories of life there with Ma and Da were breaking her heart. And now there was the misery Jack had left her with. More than once she had asked God to simply let her die.

Murph wasn't the most perceptive man in the world, but he didn't have to be hit over the head with a stick either in order to finally see that things weren't right with Grace. As much as he hoped to avoid it, Murph knew he, or someone, needed to talk to her. Eventually, he thought of Mary Miller. He'd seen her boy, Tommy, coming around checking on Grace, so he decided that it was Mary who should talk to Grace.

The next time Tommy came around, he asked him to bring his mum sometime, too. "Somethin' wrong, Murph?"

"Naw. I'm just wonderin' about Grace, is all."

"What do you mean?"

"Tommy, I don't know that I mean anything. But I'm

thinking there might be something going on with Grace, which is why I want to talk to your ma."

Tommy wasted no time. He and his ma were waiting at the front door when Murph opened the next morning.

"Hi ya, Murph. Tommy says you're wantin' to talk to me?"

"Hi Mary. Thanks for coming. I can't say I exactly *want* to talk to you, but I'm thinking I *need* to. I'm a little worried about Grace girl. Truth is, I'm more than a little worried. She just doesn't seem right. She's been through a lot lately, losing her ma and da and all. She's sure to be tired and grieving. I'm doing what I can, but I don't think it's enough. She's not looking good. In fact, she's looking a little worse every day. I was hoping you might talk to her."

"So you don't have to?"

"Well, yeah, kind of," Murph replied.

"She's upstairs now, is she?"

Murph nodded.

While Tommy waited with Murph, Mary went upstairs and knocked on Grace's door. "Grace? It's me, Mary Miller, Tommy's ma."

Grace cracked her door open, "Oh, hello, Miss Mary. Can I do something for you?"

"Well, you can start by lettin' me in."

"I'm not really prepared for company."

"I don't care about that, girl. I'm not company."

"Did Murph say something to you? What'd I do wrong?"

"Calm down, Grace. Murph's fine. You've done nothing wrong. Come on, now, let me in."

The door cracked open just enough for Mary to slip sideways into the room. It was then she saw the misery and sadness that Grace was living in while trying her best to hide them from the world. She saw the open trunk full of the things that had belonged to Grace's dead parents, as well as two small framed photos hanging on the wall. The first one was Grace as a little girl, standing in between her parents, all of them smiling as though they owned the world. The other was a formal one, her parents' wedding portrait, when they were young and still full of life. The poor lass.

"Grace, I tell you again, you're not in trouble with Murph. But he is a little worried about you. He thinks you're not doin' so well right now, and he doesn't know how to help you."

"Oh, Miss Mary, I knew it. I knew he was mad at me."

"Grace, he is not mad. He's worried. He's worried that you've had too much for one so young to deal with all by herself. And from what I'm seein', it's clear the first thing we need to do is move you out of livin' above this bar. My guess is sleep is hard enough for you to come by, and the rowdies downstairs makin' noise into the wee hours is no help. You need a break, lass. I've a spare room at my place, and that's where we're gonna take you."

Grace didn't know what to say. She was beyond grateful, but she was also undeserving. What if Mary were to find out the truth about her? What Jack had left her with? And yet, Grace knew things couldn't keep going the way they were. She also didn't know what she was going to do a few months down the road. But for now, even if it was for only one day, Grace was nothing but relieved by Mary's offer.

"Are you serious, Mary?"

"I never say things I don't mean. So, yes, I am serious."

"When ... ?"

"Well, right now, of course."

"I don't know what to say, Miss Mary. I've tried hard to get by, but I'm just so tired."

"I can see that, lass, and so can Murph."

Mary hollered at Tommy to get himself upstairs. "We're takin' Grace home with us, boy. We'll put her in the spare room. You help get her things packed up while I go tell Murph what we're doin'."

Early in the day as it was, when Mary sat down at the bar, she gladly accepted the draft Murph handed her.

"So?" was all he said.

"I'll be takin' her home with me, Murph. The girl's not well. At the very least, she needs a good, long rest and time to grieve. Can you give her some time off without firin' her outright?"

"Sure I can, Mary. She's a good girl and a hard worker, a

real hard worker. Her parents were, too. They all deserved better than they got. So, like you say, we'll give her that break, but you make sure she knows she can come back any time."

"I will, Murph. You're one of the good ones, you know."

"I'm not so sure, but thanks anyway for saying that."

"'Tis true, Murph." Mary set her empty glass on the bar and watched Tommy and Grace come down the stairs with Grace's things.

"Thanks for the beer, Murph."

"Anytime, Mary."

Grace gave Murph a goodbye hug. When she did, Murph noticed that while the rest of Grace was wasting down to skin and bones, her middle seemed to have gotten a little thick. He vaguely wondered how Grace could be losing weight everywhere else and gaining it there, especially when she ate so little. Ah, well, he decided, it was just one thing, among many, that was none of his business.

With the help of Murph's horse and wagon, it took only a few minutes to get from the bar to Mary's house. And once there, Mary again started giving orders.

"Tommy, you get Grace's things unloaded and upstairs, then take the wagon back over to Murph as quick as you can. And be sure you thank him." Mary pulled fresh linens from the closet and handed them to Grace. "Miss, your job right now is to take these sheets upstairs, make the bed and then get into it. Your rest starts right now. I need to get over to Marta's, but I'll be home after dinner there, and I'll be bringin' back somethin' for all of us to eat."

"Ma, after Murph's, you want me to go to Miss Marta's, too?" Tommy asked.

"Not today, Tommy, you take care of things here. But don't you be pesterin' Grace!"

Grace hesitated, but she had to know. "Can I ask you something, Mary?"

"Of course, anythin'."

"Jack used to come around Murphy's all the time. But I haven't seen him for a while. Did he leave town or something?"

Mary thought carefully before answering Grace's question. "Yes, dearie, he's left town. You'll not be seein' him around anymore."

"It's not that I care, you understand. I was just wondering."

"Well, sure. I get it. You see someone every day and then not at all. Of course, it makes you wonder. But, aye, he's gone for good."

"Thank you, Mary."

"Get some rest now, Grace."

CHAPTER 13

February 14, 1909

Dear Eldri,

Valentine's Day. There are so many holidays here in America that we didn't know to celebrate back in Norway.

I will use this American holiday to tell you I love you as much as ever. Wait, that's not true. I love you more than ever. Perhaps, as they say around here, absence does make the heart grow fonder. Sadly, it can also make the heart break a little with each passing day.

Your loving husband,

Ole

A ring of the front bell, and Eldri opened the door to find the most stunning spray of early spring flowers, purple hyacinths mostly, covering the top step of Marta's house.

The subtle fragrance of the flowers was heavenly. The arrangement was nearly as big as Eldri herself, or so it seemed when she lifted it into the house. She managed to carry it only as far as the entryway table.

Eldri couldn't find a card at first, and she wondered who the arrangement might have come from. John to Marta? Harry to Florence? Albert to Cissy? Perhaps Susannah had a secret admirer? Not likely. Finally, tucked deep in the heart of the arrangement, Eldri found a small card that said simply, "To M Love J." Sure she had never seen anything more romantic, Eldri went looking for Marta.

Perhaps Eldri was feeling sentimental—she didn't know—but while she and Marta were having a cup of afternoon tea together, she finally said, "Tell me how you met John."

As though she had been waiting for the day Eldri would ask, Marta began her story.

"Eldri, you first need to know that leaving you was the hardest thing I've ever done."

"But, Marta, you were so determined."

"Determined doesn't mean easy."

"Then why?"

"Had I stayed, I would have suffocated. In New York, I realized I didn't want to waste my life working in one of those grisly shirtwaist factories. And I surely didn't leave Norway and travel thousands of miles just to find myself living on another farm. The closer we got to Conway, the more I realized that's exactly what we were going to. And when we arrived, the calm that came over your face made it clear that you were home. I was not. I had no way to be sure, but I did think the home I was looking for might be in Seattle. When our train passed through here, I watched all the people coming and going with such purpose, I saw the bright lights and the life they illuminated, and I wanted to be a part of that."

Eldri didn't tell Marta the fear she'd felt in the first few hours after her sister had left, or the anger that soon followed. She'd never imagined Marta doing such a thing. But after a little time, much thought, and a very deep breath, Eldri had realized that Marta had given all she had to give. She knew Marta had taken responsibility for her all the way from Norway, across the Atlantic Ocean, through Ellis Island into New York City, and all the way across the vast country that was the United States. Eldri could take no more from Marta. And yet, here she was just two years later, dependent on Marta once again. It was humiliating.

Her thoughts returning to the moment at hand, Eldri said, "I'm still waiting for you to tell me how you met John."

Marta smiled. "All right, all right. I'll tell, but only if you tell me how you met Ole."

Eldri wasn't sure she could do that but she was curious enough about Marta and John's relationship to agree.

Pouring herself another cup of tea, Marta began her story. "I was exhausted and sad when I got on the train going to Seattle, but I didn't let myself cry until I had settled in my seat and felt the jolt of the train as it pulled away from the Conway station. I must have dozed off soon after because I don't remember anything until I opened my eyes to the sight of a gentleman, a quite handsome gentleman, sitting across from me. And he was staring right at me. Thinking something was wrong with my appearance, I straightened my hat and smoothed my skirt. I then asked the gentleman if there was something wrong. His answer was just a confused look."

"Let me guess, you asked in Norwegian."

"I did. So I tried again, in English this time. He told me there was absolutely nothing wrong. Then he said that since I was Norwegian, or at least he assumed I was Norwegian, he expected I was on my way to Ballard."

"And the gentleman was John?" asked Eldri.

"Yes, it was John. Of course, I didn't know anything about Ballard, or Seattle, for that matter. John explained that Ballard was where most Norwegians, actually most Scandinavians, in Seattle had settled. Since I didn't have a better plan, I decided Ballard was where I would at least start my new life. When we got close to the Ballard Station, John offered to escort me off the train and help get me settled."

"And you trusted him? Did you not remember the leering eyes of all the so-called gentlemen, especially those in Chicago, during our train ride on the Great Northern?"

"I certainly did remember, Elle. And because of that, my trust was not without reservation, serious reservation. But John seemed deserving of a measure of trust, and he's never proved otherwise. He is an honest and decent man."

"Except to his wife," shot Eldri.

"Careful what you say. You know nothing of the relationship he has with his wife."

Eldri's face reddened. "You are right, Marta. Let me take that back, please."

"Careful about being quick to judge, Eldri. It does not flatter."

"It does not," said a humbled Eldri. "And I apologize. Please, go on."

"No more judgments?"

"No more."

Marta continued. "John escorted me off the train at the Ballard Station. As you saw when you arrived, it's little more than what's called a 'whistle stop' with a small platform and tiny ticket booth." The sisters shared a laugh and agreed the "BALLARD" sign was just about the biggest thing to be found there.

"John flagged down a cab to take us up the hill to the St. Charles Hotel. When we arrived, he let two rooms and

escorted me to the door of my own, but not before inviting
me to dinner. He must have stayed in his room only long
enough to drop his bag and freshen up before he was back
and knocking on my door. My own bag hadn't even been on
the bed long enough to wrinkle the spread.

"We enjoyed a quiet dinner in the hotel's dining room,
and listened to the Norwegian conversations carrying on all
around us. John didn't understand most of what was being
said, but he didn't seem to care. We had a wonderful time."

"And you ate pickled herring, perhaps?"

"Ish! My attention was on the man sitting across the
table from me. I have no idea what I ate, but I do know it
did not include pickled herring. Anyway, it was quite late
when we got back to the hotel. I thanked John for a
wonderful evening, went into my room, and collapsed.

"By the next morning, both of us knew we were going to
be together in some way. John told me he'd decided he would
find a place in Ballard for me to live."

"And you were not suspicious of his intentions?"

"Of course I was! I am not an idiot, Elle! You cannot
imagine how many times in those first days I asked myself if
I could really be so lucky as to meet a true gentleman on the
train while, at the same time, reminding myself to keep a
level head."

"You did not think John was offering you a life as one of
those women?" asked Eldri.

"It might seem that way to you, Elle, but I was there. And, clearly, I did not. If you had been in my shoes, I do believe you, too, would have trusted John's intentions."

Eldri was unconvinced, but she bit her tongue and stayed quiet. She had already spoken out of turn once. She had no intention of doing so again.

"Anyway," Marta continued, noting the skeptical look on Eldri's face. "I told John I wouldn't accept charity. But, for reasons of his own, John had decided to help me. Greatly. We walked up and down Ballard looking for just the right place to start my new life and eventually found Halverson's Boardinghouse, this house. There was a second-floor room available, with high ceilings and a big, sunny window."

"That sounds like Harald's room."

"Ya, you're right. The room was perfect, and I knew I could live there. Sally Halverson looked at us a little suspiciously at first, but the look faded just as soon as she had John's generous payment of several months' advance rent in her hands. And, over time, I believe Sally's suspicions also faded. John and I both knew how our behavior could affect the reputation of her boardinghouse. As you already know, Sally is a widow, and the boardinghouse was her only means of supporting her family. We were determined not to sully its reputation, which would have been ruinous for Sally—and probably for John and me as well.

"I tell you, Elle, as certainly as I knew I wasn't meant to stay in Norway, I sensed I was finally where I belonged. That sense came with a settled feeling I'd never had before.

"It took us all day to find Halverson's, and not long after we did, it was time for John to leave for his own home. As I heard the front door close behind him, I walked over to the window and watched while his cab faded into the early evening shadows."

"John didn't tell you he was married?" asked Eldri.

"That again? No, Elle, he did not. Nor did he hide the gold band on the fourth finger of his left hand. I guess for the two days we spent together, he pretended he wasn't married, and I pretended not to notice his wedding ring. After those two days, it didn't matter anymore."

"That is not how Mor and Far raised us."

"I realize, Elle, but we don't do everything the way our parents raise us. We grow up and make our own choices. I choose to be with John, whether or not he is married. But, I remind you, we try to be discreet. John has more to lose than I do, but neither of us wants to hurt anyone by being together."

"That's all very thoughtful, but what about you? Don't you want to marry? Have children?"

"I'm not sure I do. One thing is certain, though. I would rather be with John when I can, as much as I can, than to be married and have a family with someone else."

"You love the man, Marta."

"Yes, Elle, I do." As if to shake off her story, Marta stood, stretched, then sank back into her chair.

"Now it's your turn, little sister. Tell me, who is this Ole Larsen?"

Eldri stayed silent.

"Oh no, you don't. I was honest with you. You need to be honest with me. And you especially need to be honest with yourself."

"Ya, Marta, I know. Let me think. How to describe Ole Larsen ... Well, I know Ole came from Norway several years ago. He is not tall, he does not have blue eyes or blond hair. But what he does have is kind eyes and a sturdy build. He has a look all his own that, put together, makes him unique, and rather attractive," Eldri said with a blush.

"And how did you meet Mr. Larsen?"

"I first saw him at the Conway mercantile. Mrs. Brotvik ... You remember Mrs. Brotvik?"

"Who could forget her?"

Eldri smiled, then continued. "Mrs. Brotvik had sent me to get something, but I do not remember what it was. All I remember is rushing into the store with my head down and bumping into something. Turns out, I did not bump into some *thing*, I bumped into some *one*. I nearly fell back— right on my *sete*, my behind! And I would have, too, if a pair of strong arms had not caught me."

"You really did crash into him?" Marta's hand went to her mouth, and her eyes laughed.

"Ya, I sure did. When I worked up the nerve to look at who I had crashed into, I saw the sturdy tree of a man, Ole Larsen. As it turns out, Ole is also very good friends with Alf. He is the man who married my friend, Anna, you know. Anyway, Ole and Alf work together up at the logging camp. Ole has his own horses and wagon, so sometimes he comes into Conway to get supplies for the camp and then stops at Mrs. Brotvik's for lunch. It is odd, but when I started going to the church with Anna, and then Alf, Ole soon started coming, too."

"I am quite sure that was no coincidence, Elle."

"Well, I thought it was."

"But, surely, you now know better. And you must be wondering why he thought it would be all right to marry you that day at the courthouse."

"The wondering has nearly driven me crazy."

"Then let us try to unravel the mystery and help you get your sanity back. Did anything happen before that day?"

"No. Nothing I can think of, anyway. The Sunday before was the picnic basket auction after church. Ole came in and sat down next to Alf, as usual. He took off his hat, looked over at me, and smiled. I felt my face turn bright red. And then, Anna giggled at me, loudly enough for the whole church to hear and make everyone turn to look at us, which only made things worse."

"It sounds like your Anna is a friend who doesn't take life too seriously, Elle. Those can be the best kind."

"Maybe so, Marta, but I tell you, it was a little humiliating."

"I understand. No one likes to be humiliated, you and me least of all. But we aren't going to change that about ourselves, not today, anyway. So for now, let's just worry about Mr. Larsen. Go on with your story."

"Well, at the auction, Alf won Anna's basket, of course, and Ole won mine. Alf, Anna, Ole, and I ... oh, yes, and Ole's dog, Gus ... we had a wonderful afternoon together. When we had eaten all we possibly could, Alf and Anna went for a walk. Ole and I stayed where we were, in the shade of a tremendous lilac tree, and we just talked and talked. I felt like we could have talked until the sun went down, and even into the night, and not run out of things to say. It seemed like Ole felt the same way."

"The man is smitten."

"No, he just wants a cook and a maid."

"You don't give him enough credit. Or yourself."

"I do not know what you mean."

"Well, I think Mr. Larsen sees you for the admirable young woman that you are. And I also think you miss him more than you let yourself believe."

"I admit I am very confused. When I think about Ole

before that awful day at the courthouse, I remember that he was always considerate and kind."

"How did you feel when you saw him at the church or when you brought his lunch at Mrs. Brotvik's?"

"I'm usually pretty steady, do you agree?"

"Yes, Elle, you are."

"Well, when Ole comes around, I start stumbling."

"Stumbling?"

"My thoughts get mixed up, my stomach gets tight, I do not talk right, and, once, at the boardinghouse dining room, I dropped his lunch plate right into his lap! So, yes, I stumble. Ole did not seem to mind, but Mrs. Brotvik sure got mad at me, I tell you."

"Ole Larsen, you say?"

"Yes, John."

"Well, I'll be damned. It's a small world, Marta. There's an Ole Larsen who works up at our logging camp in Conway. Well, he did work at the camp. He and his pal, a guy named Alf, quit a couple months ago to start farming."

"One and the same Ole Larsen. It was Alf's marriage to Eldri's friend, Anna, that started this whole mess."

"I can tell you, Marta, Eldri is lucky to have him in her life. And if she gives him another chance, I am sure she will find no better husband, despite how she came to be married to him."

"But what about how he tricked Eldri?"

"Marta, I've known Ole for years. There is no guile or trickery in the man. And for what it's worth, his absence is a big loss for the camp."

"I don't think Eldri knows he has left there."

"And it is not our business to tell her. Ole had his reasons, and were I to guess, I'd say Eldri had something, maybe everything, to do with it. But, believe me, Marta, the Ole Larsen I know would never intentionally deceive anyone. Somehow, he must have thought Eldri had agreed to marry him."

"Intentional or not, he did deceive her. And while I believe what you're saying, John, I think Eldri might take more convincing."

"You will not add to her confusion by telling her Ole has left the camp?"

"I will not, but I'm not happy about it."

February 19, 1909

Dear Ole,

Marta has a special man in her life, and he has given me permission to tell you who he is. But you must promise to keep it to yourself. I hope I

*can trust that you will. He is someone you know,
John Harris. He says you work for him up at
Conway, and he speaks very highly of you.*

*John is a good man to my sister. I do wish he
weren't married, but Marta says we have no
control over who we fall in love with. I wonder if
she's right.*

Affectionately,

Eldri

CHAPTER 14

March 6, 1909

Dear Eldri,

*The weather here is improving, more blue skies
than gray ones. Maybe the worst of the rain is
over, at least for now.*

*Thank you for your recent letter and for trusting
me with the news of your sister and John Harris.
Maybe that explains what happened to Harris.
Until a couple years ago, there seemed to be
something a little sad about him, especially when
he was getting ready to leave the camp and go
back to Seattle. I wondered what changed
because Harris has more enthusiasm for, well,
just about everything. I guess the change was
your sister. If that's what she's brought to
Harris's life, then good for her. The man is
honest and fair, and, despite the fact that he is
the boss, he works harder than anyone else at the
camp. I am sorry their relationship is*

*complicated, but John is a good man. I have no
doubt he will do his best for your sister.*

*Do not worry, I will keep that information to
myself.*

*I've been going to church again lately. After you
left, it was hard to go back. But Alf and Anna are
there every Sunday, and it helps me to be with
them. Everyone asks about you. They wonder
where you've gone and why. Some of the guesses
are a little funny. Others, sad. Some say you ran
off because you couldn't stand to stay at Mrs.
Brotvik's without Anna there. Some say you went
all the way up to Alaska. Some say you
wandered off and got lost up in the woods near
the town of Alpine.*

*I'm too ashamed to tell anyone the real reason
you left, and I'm grateful Alf and Anna say
nothing, either. One thing is for sure, they all
miss you. But no one misses you more than I do.*

Your loving husband,

Ole

As he slogged down to the river with Gus, Ole smiled ruefully and thought about his most recent letter to Eldri. Apparently, the grayest of days were not gone after all. The weather was wicked, the rain was coming down in sheets, and the cold was penetrating. The early morning had been a little gray perhaps, but all in all, it had looked like a good day for fishing. The rain clouds had sneaked in while Ole was grabbing up his fishing pole and tackle box. Not bothering to hitch up the horses to the wagon, he'd whistled for Gus and the two of them had headed down to the fishing shack.

Just as man and dog passed the midway point between farm and river, the rain moved in. Ole was glad to reach his fishing shack, but he knew that while it protected him in a misting rain, it was little help in a torrent. And this rain was fast becoming a torrent. "No fishing today, girl," Ole said as he scratched Gus's neck.

Concern over the rain was soon overshadowed, however, by what Ole caught sight of in the river: a piece of familiar-looking fabric wedged on a jagged branch jutting out from a half-sunken log. Then he saw the hand, and the leg with the black shoe on the end of it. Finally, the face, swollen and grotesque from its time in the water.

After losing his partially digested breakfast into the Skagit, Ole wiped his sour mouth with the cuff of his flannel shirt sleeve and tried to figure out what to do. He knew he needed help, but he also knew the swift current was threatening to lift Gudrun Brotvik's lifeless body off the log and carry it away.

Ole didn't know the depth of the water around Gudrun's body and hoped it wasn't over his head, or not by too much, because he was not a strong swimmer. But he figured the only way to find out the depth of the water was to go out there and see how far he could get. He took the rope hanging on a hook inside the fishing shack, tied one end to what looked like the best rooted tree at the riverbank, tied the other end around his waist, braced himself, and ventured into the dark, frigid water.

Gus barked incessantly. There was no way to silence her, and Ole figured if anyone happened by, her barking just might help. He couldn't count on it, though, so he kept wading, deeper and deeper, and was grateful that when he finally reached the log, the river was only halfway up his chest.

He was soaked, of course, both from the river below and the pelting rain above, but at least his arms were above the surface of the water, which made the job of untying the rope from his own waist and retying it around Gudrun's somewhat manageable. While securing her body, Ole saw it was not the fabric of her skirt but the chain from a gold locket around her neck that had caught on the jagged branch. Holding his breath, Ole gripped the rope tightly and carefully lifted the chain off the branch. The current wanted its way, but Ole managed to fight it off and hold onto the bloated form.

Ole had nearly reached the riverbank when Gus's incessant barking paid off.

"Ho, down there. Is that Gus doing all the barking? Ole, is that you? Things okay?"

"Perfect timing," Ole mumbled to himself. Then louder, "Ya, it's Gus, alright, and me. Things are not okay, and I could sure use some help."

Two loggers from the camp hurried down the slope to the riverbank.

"Fred? Hank? Boy, oh, boy, am I glad you wandered by."

"What's up, Ole? What's with all the racket Gus is making? Wait. What the hell are you doing?"

"Please, I need help. Now. It's Gudrun Brotvik. I found her in the river, and I'm trying to get her out, without drowning myself in the process. If you would stop talking and get over here, I would sure appreciate it."

The two men grabbed the line to haul Ole, and then Gudrun's body, the last few feet out of the water.

"What next?" one of the men asked through a hand-covered mouth as he tried to keep his food down and not breathe too deeply. The other, not so lucky, retched then, just as Ole had done earlier, vomited the contents of his stomach into the river. "Sorry," was all he said when he lifted his head afterwards.

Ole shrugged off the apology. "Well, I guess I need to get my wagon and take her ... where? To the sheriff? The morgue? Her boardinghouse?" Ole said through chattering teeth and shivering shoulders. Hank took off his jacket and handed it to Ole, who accepted the gesture gratefully.

Fred offered to stay behind with the body while Ole and Hank went for the wagon. "Let's just get Gudrun into the shack. It doesn't matter anymore if she gets wet, but it will keep at least some of the rain off of you, Fred," said Ole.

All the time Ole had lived at the logging camp he'd not felt a sense of camaraderie with anyone except Alf. Perhaps he'd not really given the men at the camp a chance at camaraderie. Perhaps. But one thing was sure: Now was not the time for contemplation. Now was the time to get dried off and to take Gudrun's body where it needed to go—after figuring out where that was.

When they reached the cabin door, Ole and Hank gave it several anxious knocks. Anna answered, took one look, and gestured for the men to come inside. "What's happened?"

"Where's Alf?" asked Ole.

"Alf, get over here," hollered Anna.

"Ole?" said Alf after hanging the fire's poker back on the wall and crossing the room to where Ole was standing.

"I found Gudrun Brotvik floating in the river. Hank here, and Fred, you know them, Alf ..."

"Is she ... ?" Anna's hand covered her mouth and couldn't finish. Alf put a steadying arm around his trembling wife.

"Sorry, Anna, but yes. Drowned," replied Ole.

"Where is she now?" asked Alf.

"Inside the fishing shack. Fred is with her. We need to get the horses and wagon hitched up as fast as we can and get back over there."

Recovering herself, Anna said, "First thing you need to do, Ole, is get into some dry clothes."

"No argument there, Anna. I'm sure Hank would like to have his jacket back, too, despite it being a little soggy."

Anna got some hot coffee into the chilled men and hung Hank's jacket near the woodstove that Alf had been feeding since the start of the morning's rain. Ole went to his room in the barn to change into dry clothes. As the chill on Ole's skin started to wear off, Alf and Hank came into the barn to help with the horses. Anna came with them and asked, "Ole, where are you planning to take Gudrun's body?"

"I'm not sure. What do you think?"

"The sheriff. He's the one who'll have to figure out what happened to her. He should be the first to know."

"I suppose."

With Ole in dry clothes and the horses hitched to the wagon, the men set off for their sad mission on a day that had truly turned cold and gray.

March 21, 1909

Dear Eldri,

I am sorry to write with news that I know will cause you pain.

Not long after my last letter, I found Mrs. Brotvik's body floating in the Skagit. Gus and I had gone out there for what I thought would be a good morning for fishing. But the weather turned, and I decided to go back home. Just before I left, though, something in the river caught my eye. It was Gudrun.

Luckily, a couple men from the camp wandered by. They heard Gus barking and came down the bank to help me get her out. Alf and Anna were a big help, too. We took Gudrun's body to the sheriff. He did as much investigating as he could and finally decided it was most likely she took her own life by walking into the river too far to be able to swim out, and she probably did not know how to swim anyway.

During his investigation, the sheriff found some journals that Gudrun had written. They are full of sad stories of loss, especially about her husband and young son. In some ways, I can now understand why she never seemed to warm to anyone. Perhaps she had lost so much in the life she'd had before any of us ever knew her that there was just no more room in her heart for more loss. If you don't have friends, you can't lose friends. One thing is sure: we will never know. Gudrun took the answers with her.

Anna, Alf, and I tried to do right by Gudrun. We think we did. We convinced the sheriff that there is no actual evidence her death was intentional, so he agreed to drowning as the cause on her death certificate. You know Reverend Torgersen is a good man, and he didn't want to refuse Gudrun the Christian burial we all felt she, or at least her family, would want. So she's now at the Scandinavian Cemetery up on Old Milltown Road. Hopefully, she is finally at peace.

I found a gold locket around Gudrun's neck with two miniature photos inside. Of course, the photos had gotten wet, but after they dried out, I

could see one was the image of a young man and
the other a small child. After learning what was
in her journals, it's easy to assume these were the
two people Gudrun loved most in life and who
she lost too soon—her husband and her son. I
thought about sending the locket to you, but
Anna said it was more proper that Gudrun, the
locket, and the images it contained should be
buried together.

I know you are related to Gudrun in some way. I
hope you, too, will feel we did right by her.

It is trials like these that I wish you were here to
help me through.

Your loving husband,

Ole

Eldri didn't remember covering her mouth with her hand or
know when the tears had started down her cheeks. She was
so very sad: for Ole, for Anna and Alf, and, most especially,
for Mrs. Brotvik, Gudrun. She needed to tell Marta. And she
would have to send Tante Lena the same letter of sad news
she'd just received from Ole.

March 31, 1909

Dear Tante Lena,

There is no good way to start this letter, and I cannot shield you from the sad news it contains.

Your sister, Gudrun, recently passed away. She drowned in the Skagit River, which is located not far from her boardinghouse. She was found in, and taken from, the river by a dear friend of mine. He also made sure she received a Christian burial.

There is no way to fully understand why Gudrun went down to the river, or how she went in. I hoped I would never need to tell you, but the truth is, Gudrun was desperately unhappy. I am told she left journals that tell the story of her unhappiness, especially her sadness at losing her husband and young son. I always assumed she had been married at one time, but I never knew of a child.

There was a gold locket found on Gudrun. It held

*two miniature photos, which are believed to be
her husband and son. It was buried with her.*

*As you know, I have been staying with Marta in
Seattle. But for the year that I was in Conway
and worked at Gudrun's boardinghouse, I hope
you understand I was as kind to her as I was
able.*

*Do not feel guilty that you should have done
more for Gudrun, because there is nothing you
could have done. She neither gave nor received
kindness well. My heart tells me the best way to
honor your sister is to remember her as the happy
woman in the photo you gave me and Marta,
which I now return to you.*

*Marta joins me in sending our deepest sympathy.
We cannot imagine the grief of losing your sister
because neither Marta nor I can imagine life
without each other.*

Love,

Eldri

April 6, 1909

Dear Ole,

Thank you for telling me about Gudrun. I am sure your letter was no easier to write than the one I had to write to my Tante Lena.

Marta and I were not directly related to Gudrun. Lena is our aunt by marriage. She sponsored Marta and me so we could come to America. Gudrun was Tante Lena's sister.

I am sure my tante had no idea how miserable her sister was, and I hated having to tell her. Sadly, there was no way to spare her.

I do wish letters could be filled with only happy news, but life is not filled with only happy events. So if we are to be genuine, not every letter we write will carry good news.

With gratitude and affection,

Eldri

CHAPTER 15

April 11, 1909

Dear Eldri,

God Påske. Happy Easter, my dear wife.

*The Easter Bunny? There was an Easter egg
hunt at the church after services today. How does
a rabbit supply hard-boiled eggs? I have been in
this country for many years, but how this
tradition came about remains a mystery to me.*

*Now that the weather is getting better, Alf and I
are hard at work again on that house—for Anna.*

Your loving husband,

Ole

Ole looked out over his verdant fields and the adjacent ones
that belonged to Alf. When they bought the land, they knew
the hours and hours of sweat and hard work it would take to

ready those fields for planting corn, peas, potatoes, wheat, and raspberries. But they also knew their bodies would not hold up forever against the dangerous life of logging. And they wanted to leave that life behind while they still had all their fingers and toes.

Spring had finally arrived, and with it came renewed hope. Eldri was writing him back, and her letters were growing in warmth and familiarity.

Still, on this particular morning, Ole felt a lonely gloom descending on his mood. A walk would do him good, so he pulled on his rubber work boots and opened the door of the rude cabin. "Some honeymoon castle," he muttered. "Come on, Gus."

Alf and Ole had gotten the walls up on the farmhouse, and Anna could not have moved out of the cabin fast enough. But Ole was equally glad to move into it. However primitive, it was certainly a step up from the walls he had installed for himself in the barn.

As man and dog wandered through the fields in the bright morning sun, Ole felt his dark mood start to lift. He thought about the events of the past several months, the months since his stupid, stupid mistake. He was trying to prove himself worthy of a second chance.

He wondered if Eldri's letters were opening another chance for him. He sure hoped so. "You know what, Gus? Without her, I don't give a damn about the farm, the fields, the corn, peas, potatoes, wheat, or raspberries. Without her, I am not living a life; I'm just going through the motions of one."

But she's writing you back now, and her letters are getting longer and more frequent, Ole told himself. And now she signs them *Affectionately*. Not as good as *Love*, but a whole lot better than just *Sincerely*. Ole scratched Gus's neck and let himself believe that with the day's signs of spring and new beginnings, perhaps there were signs of a new beginning for Eldri and himself as well.

April 15, 1909

Dear Ole,

A belated Happy Easter to you.

At Christmastime, Marta received a letter from our brother, Jan. Our family's farm in Rissa was in trouble. Jan made some poor decisions and would have lost the farm if Marta had not sent him the money to save it. But she did not give him the money, nor did she lend it to him. She paid off Jan's debts, and now she owns the whole farm.

At first, Jan, and especially his wife, Dagmar, refused to sell to Marta. But they really had no choice. I smile every time I think of Marta as the farm's owner and my prideful brother and his greedy wife renting from her. But mostly, I am grateful Marta saved our family from losing the house and farm, where so many memories are stored.

Thoughts of Rissa bring me to thoughts of Conway. With spring here again, I'm sure it's beautiful where you are. I suppose the lilacs are blooming. I miss my life there. It suited me, much more than life here in Seattle does.

I hope you are well and taking good care of Gus.

Affectionately,

Eldri

After reading Eldri's latest letter, Ole looked out the small, back window in the cabin and over the farm fields waiting to be worked. How could life go on as before, as though nothing had changed, when, in fact, everything had changed? The sun still came up in the morning and went down at night.

Every morning the horses, and Gus, still needed to be fed.
Ole didn't much care if he ate, but he knew it was necessary.
The light of hope was dim on this gray and lonely morning.
Eldri had taken most of it with her.

Just then, Ole saw the flowers of a wild lilac tree
rustling in a light breeze. "Come home, Eldri. Please. Come
home," he whispered to the tree. "The lilacs are blooming,
and they're waiting for you."

That same morning, Eldri looked out the window of her
little room and watched the world awaken. How could life go
on as before, as though nothing had changed when, in fact,
everything had changed? The sun still came up in the
morning and went down at night. The dresses still needed
mending, and there were school lessons to finish. Every
morning, Mary brewed the coffee and fixed breakfast. Eldri
didn't much care if she ate, but she knew it was necessary.
She carried a faint light of hope in her heart, hope that
things would be right again.

Eldri watched the delicate leaves of a tree rustling in the
light breeze and was reminded of the lilac that had shaded
her and Ole during their picnic lunch. The leaves seemed to
be whispering, "Go home, Eldri. Go home."

CHAPTER 16

May 17, 1909

Syttende Mai

Dear Eldri,

Constitution Day. An important day for Norway and us, her people.

The farmhouse is coming along and is almost finished, and Alf and Anna have moved in. I can tell you, Anna does not miss that rough cabin. Not one single bit. Alf made sure the new house is sturdy, and Anna is making it look real nice. I think it will be all finished by summer.

The other day, Alf came home with the Sears, Roebuck catalog, and you should just see Anna's face while she looks at every single page. She is beside herself picking out this kitchen stove, that washing machine, this table and those chairs, this sewing machine, that cabinet, this bureau and that bed. Oh, she knows there's no way she and Alf can buy those things, at least not yet or not all at once. But, she's having fun, just the same.

Things are pretty quiet. I do have Gus to keep me company, although she isn't talk much of a talker. Mostly she sits and stares at me with those sad, dark eyes until I take her for a walk or feed her. But don't worry. Her dog's life isn't nearly as hard as her pitiful looks might lead you to think.

The weather is turning, and we can feel summer is near. All of us up this way are happy that the wet and gray days will soon give way to the brilliant colors of summer.

Your loving husband,

Ole

Eldri took her mother's bunad out of the closet. It was one of the few things she and Marta had brought with them when they came to America. Back in Norway, Dagmar had tried to lay claim to it, saying that since she was now the family matriarch, it was rightfully hers. That was one of the few times Jan crossed his wife, and he had paid mightily for telling her that his mother's bunad belonged to his sisters. It was days before Dagmar would speak to him again.

Among Eldri's earliest memories was sitting next to Mor while she worked on the bunad and watching all those pieces—the dark blue wool skirt, vest and cap, the starched white blouse, underskirt, and apron—come together. Perhaps that's when Eldri herself began to enjoy sewing. After the various pieces were finally assembled, Mor had begun the intricate hand work that would truly complete the costume. Warming by the fire in the evening, after supper was over and the chores were done for the day, Mor would work painstakingly on the crewel embroidery patterned around the skirt's hemline, over the bodice, and on the cap. Every stitch had to be just right or Mor would pull it out and start again.

The finished product was as beautiful a bunad as either Marta or Eldri had ever seen. And Mor looked beautiful in it. Of course, she only wore it on special occasions, weddings and funerals, mostly. When Mor died, Marta honored her by wearing the bunad to her funeral. Eldri did the same for Far. But when they grew from girls into young women, it became clear the bunad should eventually go to Eldri.

Mor had not been very tall, and when Marta had dressed in the bunad for the funeral, even she had to admit she looked slightly ridiculous. The sleeves stopped well above her wrists and the hem too high above her ankles. And she simply could not keep that bodice down on her long waist. But when Eldri put it on for Far's funeral, it was as if the bunad had been made for her.

Eldri's thoughts returned to the present while she started putting on the garment's various layers. Then, she called out to her sister. "Marta, would you come upstairs and help me with something, please?"

Marta entered the room and stopped. She paused a moment. "Elle, you often look much like Mor when you are concentrating on your sewing. But now? Now you look just like her."

Eldri held out the solje that would complete the costume. "Would you mind?" she asked. Marta pinned the piece of gold and silver jewelry at the neckline of Eldri's blouse, straightened the collar, then stood back to get a good look at her little sister. "Perfect."

"When you first came here, I wondered what I would do with you. Now I wonder what I ever did without you."

"You do not have to say that."

"Elle, you of all people know me better than that. I don't say things I don't mean. Our guests would be lost without you. Or, at the very least, they wouldn't be nearly as well dressed. And your patience? It's brought a certain calm to the place."

"I am relieved not to be a burden. And I will always be grateful for knowing I had somewhere to go. We surely did not get that kindness from Jan or Dagmar."

"The way they treated us was wrong, Eldri, and something we would never do to each other. Now, isn't there a parade you're supposed to be marching in?"

"Ya, sure, ya betcha!" Eldri laughed. Marta groaned.

It had been only two years since Norway's independence from Sweden. Coincidentally, it was also only two years since the citizens of Ballard had voted in favor of annexation to the City of Seattle and the reliable source of water that came with it. Perhaps the crowd's enthusiasm for the day came partly from Norway's independence and partly from Ballard's own fierce sense of independence, despite its annexation. Whatever the reasons, the mood of the crowd was optimistic and infectious.

Eldri joined the other marchers, all dressed in their Norwegian finest, as they gathered for the parade on that sunny spring day. And yet, while she was proud to be from Norway, Eldri didn't let herself forget why she and Marta had come to America. Suddenly, her thoughts were interrupted. "Eldri! Eldri!" she heard from somewhere on the sidewalk near where she was marching.

Turning to look, she was surprised to see Marta, Susannah, Cissy, Florence, and even Mary, all of them smiling and waving the diminutive Norwegian flags they'd just bought from the nearest souvenir vendor.

"Hallo!" Eldri waved back as tears of pride, joy, and hope filled her eyes.

When the band marched down Ballard Avenue, it began playing Song for Norway; and soon both marchers and crowd had joined in singing Norway's National Anthem:

Ja, vi elsker dette landet,	*Yes, we love this country*
som det stiger frem,	*as it rises forth,*
furet, værbitt over vannet,	*rugged, weathered, above the sea,*
med de tusen hjem, —	*with the thousands of homes.*
elsker, elsker det og tenker	*Love, love it and think*
på vår far og mor	*of our father and mother*
og den saganatt som senker	*and the saga night that sends*
drømmer på vår jord.	*dreams to our earth.*
Og den saganatt som senker,	*And the saga night that sends,*
senker drømmer på vår jord.	*sends dreams to our earth.*

Cheers went up, tears flowed down, scores of flags waved with frenzy. "Hurrah for *Syttende Mai!*"

After the parade, Eldri walked back toward Marta's house. Starting up the front steps, she again heard "Song for Norway" and, as she entered the parlor, she saw Tommy at the piano.

When he finished, he looked directly at Eldri and, with

great aplomb, asked, "So, what did you think?"

"Beautifully played, Tommy. Thank you," Eldri said, her voice cracking just a little.

With a maestro's twirl of the hand, Tommy took a ceremonious bow. "You are very welcome."

Mary, too, celebrated the day by serving up a Norwegian dinner: buttered lefse, pickled herring on rye bread, lutefisk, fiskebolle, and, for dessert, rommegrot. "All this white food—flat bread, smelly fish, boiled cod, fish balls, cream puddin'," she had muttered at some point during the day. "Give me a good corned beef and boiled cabbage, I'd say. At least they have some color." Susannah, Cissy, and Florence seemed more than a little hesitant, but they were polite enough to taste the gelatinous, boiled cod smothered in melted butter. Keeping to the vow she'd made in Norway, Marta passed on the pickled herring.

What a day. But once the celebrating ended and the quiet of the night took over, Eldri's mood turned bittersweet. She remembered the beautiful summer days Ole talked about in his letter, with the sunlight that appeared early in the morning and lasted until well after supper.

Eldri began a letter to Ole. "Yes, Ole, here in Seattle, we can also tell that summer is on its way. But the sun's colors are different when reflected off city buildings rather than farm fields. And I prefer the colors of the fields. How I wish for a long walk with you across the Skagit from Conway to

Fir, and into those fields." But she gave up when a tear dropped onto the page and smeared her words.

Maybe I'm just tired and it is making me sentimental, but, Ole, I surely wish you had been here to share this day with me, Eldri thought as she rested her head on her pillow and drifted into sleep.

CHAPTER 17

That first stabbing pain of labor was inevitable, of course. "No, no. Not now." Grace hadn't been hungry for the dinner Mary had brought home that evening, and now she knew why.

From downstairs, Mary heard Grace cry out and dashed upstairs to find the girl crumpled on the floor.

"It's nothing, Miss Mary. I'm just a little dizzy. Could you help me? I think I'll lie down for a little while, and then I'm sure to feel better."

Too late for Mary to let Grace keep her secret. "I know what's what, Grace. And I know what's comin'. We'll get Tommy to heat up some water and bring some clean rags, and I'll help you get to work."

Grace struggled to talk. "Oh ... It's not what you think."

"Now, you listen to me, Grace. It's exactly what I *know*. It's exactly what I've known for months and months. Not only that, I also know how you came to be in this condition and that it is through no fault of your own."

Grace turned from Mary and started weeping. "Oh, God. I'm so sorry. And so ashamed."

"You got nothin' to be ashamed of or sorry for, Grace. It's that pig, Jack Barrett, who's to be ashamed and sorry."

"You know that, too?"

"Not much goes on around here that I *don't* know. But enough talk. We've a lot to do, and it's gonna to take all your energy to do it."

"Ahhh." In between her groan of pain, Grace managed to whisper a thank you to Mary.

"For nothin', lass. Now, stop talkin'." Mary shouted down to her son. "Tommy! Start some water boilin', lots of it, and grab the bleached rags from the top shelf in the pantry. When you've got that done, bring the stuff up here and knock on the door. I'll come out to get them. Don't you come in. What's happenin' here is none of your business."

Tommy was worried about Grace and wanted to see her for himself. But he knew better than to cross his mum and, wisely, did as he was told.

After giving Abby a cursory physical check, Mary said, "Seems this wee one is in no hurry to come into the world. Happens a lot with the first. I guess they just like being safe and sound right where they are. But that's not how it works, so we'll have to help this one on his way. Come on, now. Stand up. We need to start walkin'."

"Oh, Mary, I can't walk. It'll tear me right in two."

"You got no choice. That baby needs to come out, and you need to walk to get him out. But do not push until I tell you, no matter how much you want to. Do you understand?"

Grace could manage nothing no more than a weak nod.

Mary pulled Grace up, put her arm around her shoulder, and hauled her out of bed. "Ahhh, Mary, no!"

"It's not a choice. You've got to."

For the next two hours, Mary walked Grace in circles around the room. She finally let Tommy in because both women needed some water, and Mary couldn't leave Grace long enough to fetch it. When Tommy brought the water, Mary could tell that the sight of Grace so pale and in such pain scared him. She figured he was probably just as mad at Jack for doing this to Grace as she was, and she was glad Jack wouldn't be bothering Grace, or anyone else, ever again.

Despite his protests, Mary soon shooed Tommy out of the room, led Grace gently back to bed, and said it was time to start pushing.

"Hard, hard, harder."

The baby's head was crowning, but the rest of him wasn't coming out, so Mary told Grace, "That's it, lass. Now, one last big push!"

Holding her breath until she thought her face might burst, Grace grunted and gave that last push. The next thing either of them knew, Mary was wiping the blood and birthing fluid off the tiny baby who had been growing inside Grace for the past nine months.

"Mary, what is that blue thing?"

"That? That's the umbilical cord. It joins baby to mother

in the womb. But its work is done now." Mary took the knife Tommy had brought and severed the cord that had tied mother and baby together.

"You have a baby boy." Mary swaddled the newborn in the small flannel blanket that had once swaddled Tommy.

"A boy? And … is he okay?"

"He sure is. Ten fingers, ten toes, and all the other parts that count, too." Mary winked. "Now you get some sleep while I take care of this little one."

Tommy had sneaked back into Grace's room. Mary supposed he needed to see for himself that Grace was okay, so she let him stay, but only a moment. After making Grace comfortable, Mary turned her son around and again ordered him downstairs. "Time to leave the mother for a while. She needs some rest, I need to feed this wee one, and you need to get to cleanin' things up around here."

Tommy just said, "Yes, ma'am. Good night, Grace."

"Good night, Tommy. God bless you and your ma." Grace smiled, her first smile in a very long time.

With his arms full of soiled linens and the empty water bucket, Tommy closed Grace's door as quietly as he could, but left it ajar just enough to hear Grace if she happened to call.

While Tommy put the soiled linens in the big kettle on the stove to boil, Mary dripped spoons full of canned milk into the baby's tiny mouth. "We need to get us some bottles and nipples. Why didn't I think of that sooner, dammit?" she said out loud, then reminded herself to watch her tongue in front of the baby. Tommy chuckled at his ma. They both listened with relief to Grace's quiet breathing.

The quiet didn't last. It was soon shattered by a panicked scream. Mary quickly set the baby in the dresser drawer she had converted to a makeshift crib and raced upstairs. Tommy was already there looking at Grace rolled up in a ball, gripping her middle and writhing in pain. She was soaked in blood.

"Tommy, fetch the doctor. Hurry!" Mary told him.

"What's happening?"

"You can see things aren't right, and Grace needs more help than we can give her."

From the time Tommy left Grace's room, slammed the front door, and arrived at Doc's house, he never stopped running. He didn't know what was happening, but he did know all that blood was a bad sign.

"Doc, Doc." Tommy hollered as he pounded on the front door.

It was Doc's wife who answered. "Tommy, what's wrong?"

"It's Grace, you know, the girl from Murphy's. She's bleedin' all over the place."

"You come in, and I'll go get Doc. He'll be down just as quick as he can."

After what Tommy thought was forever, but was actually only a few minutes, he and Doc were on their way back to Mary's, both of them riding Doc's sway-backed old mare, which had faithfully seen him to and from so many emergencies over the years. Doc knew the day would come when she wouldn't be up to the task, but that was not this day.

When they walked into the house, they were met by Mary cradling the baby in her arms. "She's gone" was all Mary could manage to say. Tommy's knees buckled and he collapsed onto the floor.

"Where is she?" Doc asked.

As quickly as he had fallen, Tommy scrambled back to his feet. "Up here."

Tommy took Doc up the stairs, all the while feeling his heart breaking. He couldn't believe it. Hadn't Grace been through enough? His anger at God, life, whatever grew with every step. On the landing in front of Grace's room, Doc caught Tommy's look. "Calm down, boy. Anger will not help anything. Now, open the door, and let's see what we've got."

The flinty smell of drying blood hit them first. And then they saw the bed. Grace looked very small surrounded by that sea of brownish-red. It was hard to imagine a body could hold so much blood. Tommy hung back, but Doc wasted no time going over to Grace and taking hold of her wrist.

"Doc ..."

"Quiet! She's still with us. There's a pulse. It's awfully faint, but it's there. If we don't get some blood into her pretty damned fast, though, she won't be with us much longer."

"Tell me what I can do."

"Roll up one of your sleeves."

"What?"

"Do as I tell you, boy. Roll up your sleeve. Grace needs some of your blood." Doc knew he was taking a big risk. "We're going to do a blood transfusion. I warn you, it's not usually successful. So don't get your hopes up. But if we don't try it, Grace will die for sure, and I'll be damned if I'm going to stand by and let another young woman die of childbirth hemorrhage without trying everything I can. You got that sleeve rolled up yet?"

"It's up."

"Good. Start pumping your hand in and out of a fist."

Tommy didn't understand what was going on, but he wasn't about to waste precious time by asking a bunch of stupid questions, and simply did as he was told.

Mary had come into the room by then, carrying the new baby. With Tommy and Mary looking on, Doc moved the only chair in the room as close to Grace's bed as he could get. He then opened his bag and pulled out a three-foot length of rubber tubing and two large glass syringes.

Tommy's eyes grew wide when he saw the syringes, which seemed to be the size of the billy clubs the cops carried on Ballard Avenue, and the equally intimidating needles Doc was attaching to them.

Doc ignored Tommy's reaction. "Sit here." He pointed to the chair. Then he wrapped the rubber tube around Tommy's upper arm and made a tight knot in it. "Keep opening and closing your fist."

"Okay, enough," and Doc quickly inserted one of the needles into the fattest vein he could find. When he'd filled the syringe, he withdrew the needle from Tommy's arm and slapped a small square of gauze over the opening to absorb any residual blood flow. There was no fat vein in Grace's thin arm, but Doc's years of experience served him well, and, after checking the syringe for any air bubbles, he gently inserted the needle into the best vein he could find. He slowly pushed the plunger down and watched Tommy's blood empty out of the syringe and into Grace's pale body.

"I think she needs more, Doc."

"Probably so, boy, but we need to see if she tolerates this first transfusion well enough before we think about doing another."

Doc thought he saw a little color coming back into Grace's face and some twitching in her arm. Tommy was sure he saw them.

"Mary, you go downstairs now. Take care of yourself and

that little one. You have anything to feed him?" Doc asked.

"I've been givin' him some of that Carnation milk. You know, that stuff in the cans?"

"Good."

"Can't say I feel right about leavin' right now."

"Tommy and I've got this. You know as well as I do, that baby is going to wake up long before you're ready for him to. And we're going to need you to take care of him. So ... go."

Mary wasn't usually one to do as she was told. She was better at giving orders than taking them, but she knew Doc was right. With a promise they would call her if anything happened, Mary dragged her tired body down the stairs and carefully tucked her charge in the open dresser drawer before lying down next to him in her own bed. Very soon, Doc and Tommy could hear Mary's heavy snores of sheer exhaustion, snores that made them both chuckle, in a night that had, thus far, lacked any humor.

"What do we do now, Doc?"

"Now, son? Now we wait. And while we're waiting, you tell me how Grace came to be in this state."

Tommy brought a chair from downstairs so he and Doc would both have a place to sit while they kept vigil.

When Tommy finished telling Grace's story, Doc said, "Jack Barrett. I might have guessed. Nothing but trouble, that one."

"Yeah. Trouble, for sure. Especially for Grace. Damn

him. And damn me for not for not going with her to the market that day."

"There was no way for you—or Grace—to know what Barrett intended. Your minds don't think that way—be glad of it. And, if you have been with Grace on that awful morning, Jack would have simply waited for his next opportunity."

"Still, it shouldn't have happened."

"No argument there. But the blame is fully on Barrett, not you or Grace. Remember that, Tommy."

"I'll try."

Man and boy spent the rest of the night alternating between dozing off, catching themselves before falling onto the floor, and checking on Grace. When Doc took her pulse, Tommy would look for other signs of life. For hours they also watched for signs of chills and fever in reaction to the transfusion but saw nothing except Grace's shallow breathing and weak, but now steady, pulse.

"Looks like she's doing okay with that first one, Tommy. If you're up to it, I want to fill that second syringe."

"I'm up to it."

"Good boy." Doc knotted the rubber tubing around Tommy's arm and picked up the second syringe while Tommy opened and closed his fist.

"Easier going this time," Doc said as he slowly injected the second syringe of blood into Grace's arm.

CHAPTER 18

Tommy and Doc had both dozed off when, near dawn, they heard a loud sigh. They woke to see Grace's open eyes.

Grace tried to sit up. "What's happened? Doc, why are you here? Tommy? Wait, where's the baby?" she cried.

"Calm down, Grace, and lie back. You're very weak. In fact, we're all very weak. Well, except perhaps for that baby of yours. Right about now, he's probably the strongest among us."

Mary was better, too, for having managed a few hours' sleep. She was in the kitchen warming yet more canned milk for the hungry little one when she heard Grace's voice. "Thanks be to God," she said, making the sign of the cross.

Rumpled and sleep deprived, Mary nevertheless got upstairs as quickly as she could and with the baby. "Here, here he is, mother. Safe, sound, and hearty," Mary said as she held out the newborn.

Grace took the baby into her arms, and then saw him, really saw him, Jack's baby, for the first time. "Take him away!" she cried.

There was nothing to say. Mary, Tommy, and Doc all knew what Grace saw. It wasn't the little one's fault, of course, but it was there nonetheless. Staring up at Grace was the very likeness of Jack Barrett.

Reluctantly, Mary did what Grace asked and took the little one back into her arms, leaving Grace sobbing into Doc's own arms. "Will it never end? God takes away my da and then my ma. He lets Jack have his way and then leaves Jack's shadow to haunt me. Why is God tormenting me? Why do I deserve this? I don't understand."

"God does not torment, my girl," Mary said. "You have indeed been through more than what you should at your young age, and you have done nothin' to deserve it. But first things first. Let's get you cleaned up, give you some food and then settle you back into bed. I won't let you even try getting' up until at least tomorrow mornin'. We very nearly lost you, and ..."

"I'm thinking it would have been better if you had. I'd now be with my ma and da and not facing a life raising Jack's boy."

"Those of us in this house would disagree with you, dear Grace. Your absence from here would leave a hole that no one else could fill. Listen to me: You must rest. Think about nothing. There is plenty of time to make a plan. The hardest, and worst, are now behind you," Doc said.

In the corner of the room, Tommy's quiet presence went unnoticed, but he'd heard every word that had just been said.

Doc went downstairs to Mary's kitchen, where she had a hot cup of coffee waiting for him. "Sit," she told him. Mary was back in charge.

"You do know she cannot keep that baby, don't you, Mary?" Doc asked.

"I was afraid of that, but I didn't want to think about it yet," she responded.

"She's much too young to be a mother, and she's much too weak to even care for herself at the moment. And she's right—the baby looks just like Jack. He will be a constant reminder of what she's been through."

"I know that, Doc. But I don't know what to do about it."

Tommy came into the room and said, "I'll take the baby to the Children's Home and leave him on the steps."

"You can't do that. He won't be safe," his mother replied.

"I'll not leave until I see he's found and taken inside."

"And what do we tell Grace?"

"It's simple, Ma. The baby died," Tommy said.

The painful discussion continued for a while longer. But in the end, all agreed Tommy's plan was the best they could come up with. Doc filled out the birth certificate, Mary cleaned up the innocent, wrapped him back in Tommy's blanket, and gently placed him in the vegetable basket that usually made its home on the back porch. When Tommy left for the Children's Home, a palpable sadness, for Grace and the baby, lingered in the air at Mary's house.

In the meantime, ignorant of the plan conspiring below her, Grace was getting her first real sleep since Jack had raped her all those months ago.

While Doc rode the old mare home, he couldn't help second guessing what he, Mary, and Tommy had done and hoping they had made the right choice. Should they have let Grace decide whether or not to keep the baby? Or had they done her a service by taking that decision from her? She had already been through so much in her young life. An orphan herself, should Grace also be saddled with mothering the issue of the violence committed against her? Doc knew Mary and Tommy might be willing to help, but life wasn't easy for them, either. Just getting by in this world was challenge enough for anyone. When Doc walked through his front door after that long night, he gratefully accepted the loving hug and warm breakfast his wife had waiting for him.

In the early morning, Sarah Carson, Matron of the Children's Home Society, opened the door of the orphanage to the sight of another basket abandoned on its stoop. She looked into the street, glimpsed a shadow at the end of the alley, and watched while it turned the corner and disappeared. Sighing aloud, she then picked up the basket, looked at the sleeping little one, and went inside. This one's plight was not unique, and the Home was full. What to do, though, but make room for one more? She soon saw the note pinned on the blanket. It read, "His name is Ernest."

"Ernest it is, then," Sarah said as she took the baby from the basket and gave him a warm hug.

Grace slept through the next day and night and finally awoke the second day after she had given birth. "Mary! What's happened?"

Mary came running up the stairs as quickly as her stout body would allow. "Oh, lass. You've been through a terrible time. Doc saved your life. Well, with a little blood from Tommy. And you've been asleep for nearly two whole days."

"And the baby?"

"My heart aches to tell you we lost the little one. He fought hard, but he just didn't want to stay in this world with us. He's with your ma and da now. They'll take good care of him."

"What? Mary, no! I saw him! I held him! You said he was fine," cried Grace.

Just then Tommy came into the room. He took Grace's hand and said, "We did all we could, Grace, but he wasn't strong enough to hang on. I am so, so sorry."

"Where is he, then? What did you do with him?"

"Doc took him when he left. He said he would take care

of things," Mary said.

Grace's mind was a mix of confusion and conflict: sadness that a new little one wouldn't get a chance at life, relief that she wouldn't be raising a baby she neither wanted nor was ready to care for, and an overwhelming feeling of guilt.

"He died because he knew he wasn't wanted," she cried.

Mary hugged her, "No, no, that's not what we did ... uh ... what happened."

"What do you mean?" asked Grace.

"Well, I mean ... I mean that he didn't die because he wasn't wanted. Yeah, that's what I mean."

"I'm confused. You're not making any sense, Mary."

"Jesus Christ, Ma. You never could keep a secret," Tommy said.

"What are you talking about?" Grace asked, turning to Tommy.

"Aw, hell, Grace. The truth is, I took the baby to the Children's Home yesterday morning. You were so weak and sad. We—Ma and me—figured if having the baby didn't kill you, raising Jack's baby would. So we did what we thought was best for you, and the baby, too. I waited around the corner until I saw a lady, who looked like she was very nice, take him in. Please don't hate us."

Grace tried to focus and hear, really hear, what Tommy was telling her. Suddenly, her breathing became fast and shallow, and she couldn't control it. And she felt as though her heart was going to pound right out of her chest. "What's happening?" she gasped.

Mary rushed over to Grace and held her tight. "Breathe, slowly, breathe, slowly, that's a girl. You're fine. You're just overwhelmed, body and spirit."

When she could finally talk again, Grace said, "The baby is the innocent in this."

"The baby is one innocent in this. You are the other," Mary replied.

Grace started sobbing. Was it possible there was a family out there who would give Jack's baby, her baby, a good life? She wanted to think so. She hadn't quite lost all hope that things might get better, but she was very, very close.

"We know this is difficult, dearie. But you need to take care of yourself so you can heal. Let me bring you some warm broth," said Mary.

"I don't want any broth, and I don't care if I do heal. What does it matter, anyway? I couldn't save my parents, and I'm not worthy of being a mother, either."

Tommy sat on the bed and held Grace. "Oh, Tommy, I miss my ma and da, I miss the life I had with them, I don't know what to do without them and now there's the baby."

"You're strong, Grace, or you will be soon enough. Then you'll make a plan. Life will be good again. You'll see,"

Tommy said.

"Maybe so. But all I am right now is sad, confused, and so very alone." Tears pooled in Grace's eyes. "I suppose there's nothing to do but get back on my feet and go back to work, if Murph will have me, that is. Please go away, Tommy. I don't want to be with anyone."

Tommy could keep quiet no longer. He put his hand on Grace's chin and turned it toward his own face. "Look at me! It's true your parents are gone, and that's terrible. But don't you understand that you did everything, everything, to save them? Sadly, it was their time. It was not your time. And as far as being worthy of motherhood, there is no one more worthy. But you deserve to become a mother when you're ready for it, not when that son of a bitch, Jack Barrett, forces it on you. And, last of all? I will not go away."

Mary watched while Tommy comforted Grace as she cried for her parents, her baby, and herself. My son, Mary thought with a smile. Might I be gettin' a glimpse of the man you will become one day? Then, her thoughts returning to more practical matters, she went downstairs to warm that broth. "I'll make Grace eat, if it's the last thing I do!" she muttered, maybe aloud, maybe only to herself.

Doc came to visit Grace every day for a week. He was pleased to see her steadily getting stronger.

"I don't have to tell you that we very nearly lost you. And we would have, if not for the transfusion from Tommy."

"So I owe him my life?"

"You do, indeed."

"Just one more way Tommy, and his ma, have saved me. I'll be a long time repaying."

"Good people don't do good in order to be repaid, Grace. You needed help, and you deserved it. There are a lot of good people out there. This time, Tommy and Mary happened to be the good people around to help you."

"And you, Doc. You're a good one, too."

"Just doing my job, miss," Doc said with a wry smile.

"I think better, and more, than most would have. Thank you."

"You are welcome, dear," he said, more seriously this time.

When Doc got downstairs, he congratulated Mary and Tommy. "Well done, both of you. Grace's vital signs are stable, and her recovery could not be going better. But the girl is too thin. Can you fatten her up a little, Mary?"

Patting her own ample stomach, Mary responded, "If anyone can do that, Doc, it's me."

"Well, perhaps not quite so earnestly as you do for yourself." He smiled. Ever since he'd know her, Doc had been trying to get Mary to lose some weight. To no avail.

"I know what to do. Coffee? It's fresh," she said.

"Yes, you do. Coffee sounds good. Thanks."

"I've recently heard Jack Barrett met with his demise," Doc said, taking a slow swallow of the hot liquid.

"Yeah, pity that," Mary said.

"Know anything about it?"

"Me? Naw. All's I know is a lot of people like Grace and a lot of people hated Jack. He was a blight on this good earth, and I don't think anyone will miss the malicious presence he disguised with his smarmy charm. He was cruel and nasty and full of himself. Good riddance, I say."

"Tempted as I am to agree with you, it would be unprofessional of me, so I won't. But I will say, I won't miss him. Nor will I miss patching up all the poor folks who dared cross him. Anyway, I'd best be off. It's nearly suppertime, and I'm ready to be home. I say again, you two are taking good care of that girl. Thank you. She deserves it. She's been through a lot. Remind me, she's how old?"

"Sixteen. Just turned."

"My God. Too young, much too young."

"Indeed. Have a good evenin', Doc. Say hello to that wife of yours."

"Will do. Thanks, again, for the coffee. Goodbye, Mary."

"Bye, Doc."

CHAPTER 19

On June 1, 1909, at 8:30 AM, the gates of the Alaska Yukon Pacific Exposition opened to the public. Because John had made a generous investment in the venture, he was able to give opening-day tickets to Marta and Eldri. He also sent a cab to Holm House very early that morning to take them east from Ballard, through several of the other new neighborhoods north of Seattle's central core—Fremont, Phinney, and Wallingford—and onto the new grounds of the University of Washington.

A gray sky threatened to dampen the day, but it didn't dampen the sisters', or anyone's, mood. When they arrived at the A-Y-P's main gate, Marta and Eldri were escorted past the crowds and through a private entrance. Much to their delight, John had not only given them opening day tickets but also VIP passes.

"VIP, Marta?" asked Eldri.

"Very Important Persons," Marta responded with a smile.

"Well, would you look at us, Marta Holm? Far and Mor could never even have imagined." The sisters locked arms and went into the Fair just as a huge shadow crossed overhead.

"Elle, look up. A flying machine!"

Holding a hand over the crown of her best hat to keep it from flying off, Eldri gazed skyward at the airship and resisted the temptation to duck her head. "It is wondrous." Then, looking all around, she said, "It's all wondrous. So many things we have never seen before. But where to start? What to do first?" She repositioned her hat, making sure its row of red roses was properly placed to the front, and looked at her program, pleased that she could read it—well, most of it, anyway.

"I say we start with the fun! Come on, Elle!"

The sisters wound around to the boardwalk called the Pay Streak. Along the way, they passed the Chinese Village and the Eskimoes, the Streets of Cairo, and the widely advertised Igorotte Village. There was the Dixieland, the House Upside Down, and the Pianotorium. They skipped the reenactment of the battle between the *Monitor* and *Merrimac*, then walked past the Spanish Theater and Temple of Palmistry.

Finally, they sat down to coffee at the Baby Incubator Café. But when they gave real thought to where they were, they found it terribly unsettling.

"I don't think I like it here, Marta. Look at those poor babies. On display as though they are sideshow freaks."

"They're in 'incubators,' Elle, which are supposed to be a big help for weak and early babies."

"I understand, but those babies look neither weak nor early. They just look like exhibits to stare at. I suppose there's nothing actually wrong with it. Still, I find it unkind and disturbing."

Marta and Eldri didn't stay long enough to finish their coffee. It had turned bitter.

"Please don't let this one thing ruin your day."

Eldri took her sister's arm. "Nothing could ruin this day. Still, I am glad to get away from that place."

Shortly before noon, Marta and Eldri walked up Union Avenue toward the Grandstand for the official opening. Among the dignitaries seated on the stage were the Exposition's major investors. All were waiting for President Taft, from behind the desk of his White House office, to wire congratulations, via a gold-plated telegraph key, to the State of Washington on the occasion of its first world's fair.

"Look at this, Marta," Eldri said, pointing to her program. "Mr. James Hill is about to speak. Maybe we should stay to hear him, because, after all, it was his trains that brought us here to Seattle."

Marta wasn't listening to Eldri. Her eyes were fixed on John, who was sitting among the other investors. Marta presumed the woman next to him, someone Marta was seeing for the first time, was John's wife, Charlotte. Even from a distance, she could understand why John's life at home was so empty. Charlotte's eyes were vacuous and cold.

Marta was certain this was a woman who would find no
fault with exhibiting orphans at a fair. On the other hand,
John looked miserable, and Marta was miserable for him.
She couldn't imagine the John she knew being married to a
woman like Charlotte. Then, just as Marta was about to look
away, she caught John's gaze and saw the trace of a smile
move across his face.

Eldri tracked Marta's gaze. "Is that John's wife? She's
certainly smiling wide."

"Yes, from what John says, this is exactly the type of
event she enjoys. She's quite social."

Marta took Eldri's arm. "Come on. I don't want to stay
here. Let's go see what the Swedish Building has to offer a
couple of Norwegians."

After lunch with the Swedes, Marta and Eldri wandered
down the cascading falls that fed the Arctic Circle, which
formed the center of the A-Y-P grounds. The Circle was
surrounded by the Agriculture Building, the Manufacturers
Building, and the Japan, Canada, European, and Oriental
Buildings. Just north of the Circle was the cornerstone of
the A-Y-P: the U.S. Government Building. Appropriately,
the Alaska Building and the Philippines & Hawaii Building,
the two other principalities that made up the "Alaska Yukon
Pacific Exposition" were situated on either side of the
Government Building.

At the end of the day, when they could walk no longer,

Marta and Eldri gave in to their protesting feet by returning to the Arctic Circle and sitting beside the edge of the reflecting pool. Their day would have ended perfectly had they been able to take in the breathtaking view of Mount Rainier. But, alas, rain continued to threaten, and its accompanying clouds masked the mountain.

"Oh, Marta, what a day this has been. Please thank John for me."

"As a matter of fact, John is coming over later tonight, so I'll have a chance to do just that."

"I think you're being naughty."

Marta simply smiled.

The sisters locked arms, as they had done so often during this day of wonder. And just as it was ending—after they exited the stiles and hopped onto the streetcar that would take them back to Ballard—the rain that had threatened all day finally materialized.

John's arrival home was even more unpleasant than usual. Charlotte had left the A-Y-P earlier in the day to organize the night's dinner with John's parents. As soon as John crossed the threshold of his Capitol Hill mansion, the unpleasantness began. His welcome home was a shrill rebuke. "Where have you been, John Harris? You were supposed to be back hours ago. I've been sick with worry."

"No, Charlotte, a bit inconvenienced perhaps, but sick with worry? I doubt it."

She ignored his comment, "Your parents are arriving any minute, and nothing has been done."

"Charlotte, I see the table is set, I'm sure the food has been impeccably prepared, and you look beautiful. What's left to be done?"

"Never mind. Please, just go make yourself presentable."

"With pleasure, Charlotte," John said as he tipped his hat and bowed mockingly.

While dressing for dinner, John started wondering what had brought on Charlotte's latest temper. But his thoughts were soon interrupted by the sound of his parents coming through the front door; his father's deep, and very loud, voice was hard to miss.

"Halloo, Harris family!" Phillip Harris boomed as John's mother, Eleanor, tried to shush her husband. She was always trying to shush him, generally a futile effort.

When John came out of his room, his two small children ran smack into him. "Daddy! Here you are!"

"I am, indeed, and how very happy I am to see you both!" He knelt to give his children a warm hug.

"Here, let me take you to your room," John said as he held out his hands.

Five-year-old Michael took his father's left hand, while three-year-old Margaret took the right. John walked down the hall with his children while their nanny waited with her hands folded over her apron and a calm smile on her face. In the nursery, John listened to their prayers, gave each of his children a goodnight kiss, and walked out of the room, quietly closing the door behind him. He nodded to the patient nanny and, as if to fortify himself, took in a deep breath before going downstairs, where his wife and parents were waiting for him.

After a hearty handshake with his father, a courteous hug to his mother, and a glare from his wife, John escorted his parents and Charlotte into the ornate dining room. John hated this room. The crystal chandelier, French of course, the heavy mahogany table with its twelve chairs, the English bone china, and the sterling flatware. It reflected everything that John was not. It had no warmth, no character. Rather, it was cold and sterile. It was a reflection of Charlotte, the Charlotte hidden from John until after he'd married her. Charlotte loved the room every bit as much as John hated it. And whenever John could stand to look at the huge, icy chandelier that Charlotte had insisted on, he couldn't help comparing it with the warm, rose-glass one he'd given Marta.

Naturally, the dinner's conversation centered on highlights of the A-Y-P Opening, who was there, and, even more interesting, who was not. Charlotte told John's mother how cute the little babies looked in those clear plastic boxes—what were they called, again? "Incubators," Eleanor had replied.

"Oh, that's right. Odd word, don't you think?" Charlotte said.

"Mmm," was Eleanor's only response.

"It's too bad about the rain tonight. The lights silhouetting the buildings couldn't be turned on," said Phillip.

"The exposition is going to be around for a while, Dad. Plenty of opportunities for the lights."

"I suppose. Hey, I nearly forgot! I brought a copy of the President's telegram." Phillip pulled a folded paper from his inside pocket.

Charlotte rolled her eyes as a proud Phillip read, in his most officious voice,

THE WHITE HOUSE

JUNE 1, 1909

MR. J. E. CHILBERG, PRESIDENT ALASKA-YUKON-PACIFIC EXPOSITION, SEATTLE, WASH.

I CONGRATULATE YOU AND YOUR ASSOCIATION ON THE AUSPICIOUS

OPENING OF THE ALASKA-YUKON-PACIFIC
EXPOSITION AND I CONGRATULATE THE
PEOPLE OF THE GREAT NORTHWEST ON
THE COURAGE AND ENTERPRISE THEY
HAVE SHOWN IN BRINGING IT FORTH.

-- WILLIAM H. TAFT"

"What do you think of that?" Phillip said. "The President says we're courageous and enterprising."

"Nothing we didn't already know about ourselves, eh, Dad?"

"Hah! Speaking of enterprise ... John, tell me about the work up north. What's the logging season looking like?"

"It's looking good. The trees are healthy and, as you know, demand remains high. Seattle isn't going to stop growing, at least not any time soon. We should have an excellent season."

"Glad to hear it. Too bad you have to spend so much time away from the family, John, but it's important for someone to be in charge up there and keeping an eye on things."

"I understand, and I agree. The trips are crucial, and they need to be frequent. In fact, I'm thinking it may be necessary for me to travel even more often than I've been doing."

Charlotte shot John a daggered look that was impossible

to miss, but it did leave him mystified. Not for long, though, because no sooner had John's parents left than Charlotte was on him, as usual, about how in the world his mother manages to put up with his boorish father.

"Charlotte, leave it." But, in typical fashion, she did not.

When John had finally had enough, he said, "Charlotte, who do you think is responsible for this house you live in, the grand furniture with which you're surrounded, the fine clothes you're constantly buying, and the very food on your table? My father. And you would do well to remember that." He started toward the front door.

"I am not finished, John Harris."

"What else can there possibly be, Charlotte?"

"Who is she?"

"What are you talking about?"

"The woman who was smiling at you with such *affection* this afternoon. It was common and truly disgusting."

"Leave it, Charlotte."

"Who is she?"

"It is none of your concern."

"It most certainly is my concern."

"Listen carefully, Charlotte, because I'll say this only once. Do you enjoy your grand life? If so, *do not* pursue this conversation any further."

"Oh, ho. Do not threaten me, John Harris. I could ask if you enjoy the company of your children."

"Charlotte, you know as well as I that we are in a loveless marriage. And we are at an impasse. I will not leave you because I love my children too much. You will not leave me because you love this life too much. I'm going out. Don't bother waiting up for my return, not that you ever would."

John put on his hat and walked out the front door, leaving Charlotte standing alone at the base of her grand staircase.

CHAPTER 20

For the first time in a very long time, Grace thought maybe
things were going to be okay. She stepped out into the
sunshine and looked up at the bluebird sky so common on a
July morning in Seattle. A tentative smile crossed her face
as she hoped that maybe, just maybe, it would be possible
for her to be happy again.

She walked toward Broadway, Ballard's main street, the
wind blowing through her long, wavy hair. It felt good. It felt
familiar. It felt normal.

All was fine, better than fine, in fact, until Grace crossed
in front of the library and saw where it had happened. The
disorientation and wave of nausea that came over her
buckled her knees, and she thought she was going to be sick.
But she caught herself instead, turned, and staggered back
in the direction of Mary's house.

In the meantime, Tommy had come home from Marta's
to check on Grace and was alarmed to find her gone. He sat
on the stoop to wait, and eventually saw her rounding the
corner. He watched as she suddenly stopped, clutched her
middle, and looked up at the sky.

The only thing keeping Grace upright was the south wall of the drugstore, but she was doing a slow slide down to the sidewalk. Tommy ran over to catch her.

"Grace! What's wrong? Where have you been?" Tommy grabbed ahold of Grace's arms as she tried to stand.

"Oh. Tommy. I'm okay. Really. I just went for a walk, is all," Grace said, trying to smile.

"I don't believe you."

"I did. I went for a walk. Only I went in the wrong direction. I was okay until I got to the library, and then a feeling came over me. I can't explain it. One minute I was fine, and then the next ... "

"Aw, God, Grace, I'm so sorry. You shouldn't go out alone. At least not yet. And you sure shouldn't go in the direction of the library."

"I appreciate what you're saying, Tommy, but I have to get on with things. And who do I have, but myself, to do it with?"

"You have me, Grace."

"You? Tommy, you're sweet to say that, but you're a boy."

Tommy was patient, especially when it came to Grace, but that remark stung him sharply. "A boy, you say? I'm but a year younger than you, Grace. And more, whose blood do you think is running through those veins of yours? Mine, that's who. And let me tell you, giving up blood isn't something a boy normally does, at least not unless he's in a fight—and it's one he's losing."

Grace started to cry. "I'm so sorry, Tommy. You're right. And I'm grateful. I really am. It's just, I'm all I have right now. I needed to step back into the world, and I failed."

"You're wrong about both, Grace. One, you are most definitely not all you have. Haven't Ma and I shown you that? And two, you don't need to step back into the world until you're good and ready. And when you do that stepping, I'll be right there with you."

Grace took a curious look at Tommy. It seemed the last time she'd looked at him, he was the kid who had followed her to market. But now? There was something different about him. "I am lucky to have you on my side, Tommy Miller. And your ma, too. I don't know where I would have gone if your ma hadn't taken me in. I'm pretty sure I'd be dead—and the baby, too," Grace said.

Tommy couldn't, or simply didn't, stop himself. He put his arms around Grace and gave her a hug—the hug he'd wanted to give her for what seemed forever. And Grace let herself melt into it, but only for a moment.

"Well, there, now, what would your ma say if she were seeing this?" Grace stiffened and stepped back, straightened her spine, then smoothed her hair and skirt.

"Ma's not here."

Tommy left Grace at the house, with a promise that she

wouldn't go out alone again. It was an easy promise to make. The episode had tired her, and she was looking forward to resting until Tommy and Mary came home that evening.

Back at Marta's, Tommy found his ma in the first place he looked for her: the kitchen, of course. After hearing what had happened, Mary said, "I suppose we should have expected somethin' like this. From now on, Tommy, you'll bring her over here when you come in the mornings. She can keep the table set and help me in the kitchen. I'll talk to Marta. In the meantime, see those potatoes over there? They aren't going to peel themselves."

Mary had an idea. She saw how hard Eldri was working to keep up with the mending the ladies at Marta's were constantly bringing to her, especially Cissy and Susannah. It occurred to her that Eldri could use some help. As far as Mary knew, Grace didn't have much, if any, experience at sewing, but there seemed to be something about the way Grace moved in the world that was similar to Eldri's. Perhaps it was the way they were both quiet and reflective, or perhaps it was their attention to detail. In any case, Mary figured that with Eldri to train her, maybe Grace could become nearly as skilled at sewing as Eldri herself. If Mary's idea worked, Eldri would get the help she needed and perhaps Grace wouldn't have to go back to Murphy's.

"Good mornin', Eldri. How goes your day?" Mary asked.

"Oh, you know, Mary, there's always something that needs mending. I'm not complaining, but there's just so much more than I can get to," Eldri replied in her best English.

"You know the girl, Grace, who's stayin' with me and Tommy?"

"You've mentioned her, ya. We've not actually met, though. Is she all right?"

"Truth is, Eldri, she's not been all right for quite some time. But she's on her way to gettin' better now. She was workin' at Murphy's Bar, but she's been weakened and shouldn't go back to the heavy work she was doin' there."

"I'm sorry to hear that, Mary. Is there anything I can do to help?"

"Maybe so. It seems to me that you could use some help with all the sewin' and mendin' you're doin' here. And I'm pretty sure Grace would be good at that."

"Oh? Does she sew?"

"I don't really know. But I do know she's patient and a hard worker. I was kinda hopin' you'd be willin' to teach her. Think about it, would ya'?"

"No need, Mary. I have received much kindness, especially here at Marta's, and I have it to give. When Grace is ready, you bring her here. I'll teach her what I know, and

I'll be very glad for the help, too."

"You won't regret it. I swear."

"No swearing necessary, Mary. I'm sure I will not regret it."

As she dressed for the day and pinned up her hair, Grace was surprised how much she was looking forward to getting out of the house. Except for that fateful walk, she had been inside for over a month. When Tommy and Mary weren't around, her days were long and sad, and filled with self-doubt. She was afraid what folks were thinking of her, after having the baby and all, especially that mean busybody, Mrs. Jorvig.

The more Grace's health improved, and the better she felt, the more she had dreaded the thought of going back to working at Murphy's Bar. Murph had been as good to her as anyone could have been, but she hated the work. Worse than that, she missed her parents every time she looked behind the bar and saw Da wasn't there or looked upstairs and knew Ma wouldn't be waiting for her. Last night's conversation, when Mary told her Eldri would teach her how to sew, came as a blessed relief. "Oh Mary, you can just know I won't let you down. I'll work until my fingers bleed," a grateful Grace had said.

"Gad, no. You bleed on those fancy dresses, and it'll be

the Dickens for me to get the stains out," Mary had
responded.

Tommy came around at mid-morning, as planned. He
found Grace sitting at the kitchen table with her straw
boater pinned on her head and her cotton coat draped over
the chair next to her. She was just finishing her morning
cup of tea, and she was the most beautiful sight Tommy
Miller had ever seen.

"Ready, Grace?" he asked, holding out a hand to help her
from the chair.

"I think so, Tommy. To tell you the truth, though, I'm a
little afraid. Do I look all right?" she asked.

"You are beautiful." There. Tommy had finally said it out
loud.

Grace blushed.

"But, come on, I need to get back."

"Am I getting you into trouble?"

"Naw. Grace, you can't get me into trouble. It's just that,
the more chores I do at Miss Marta's, the fewer Ma has to do
herself. She works too hard."

"I hope I can be some help, too."

"You like peeling potatoes?"

True enough, there was always something that needed doing
at Marta's. On that first day, in between peeling those

potatoes, setting the dining room table, dusting the front rooms, and sweeping the floors, Grace looked over at the beautiful dresses waiting to be mended.

Eldri eventually pulled Grace aside. "Mary tells me you might be interested in helping with these, Grace."

"Yes, yes I would. I don't sew much, mostly buttons and hems, but I do like it," Grace replied as she gazed at the silk and lace garments in Eldri's mending basket.

"Then sit down next to me, and we will get you started. The ladies upstairs are lovely people, but they are very hard on their clothes, especially Cissy. I do not know how she does it, but something is always giving out, popping off, or splitting open."

CHAPTER 21

"What are you saying, Mr. Coyne?"

"Just this, Matron. On Exhibitors' Day at the A-Y-P, the Alaska Yukon Pacific Exposition, as it were, they're planning a series of raffles: a cow, a rabbit, a wagon, a horse, even a whole farm. Why not a baby? Why can we not get the same publicity and recognition that the farmers, loggers, and carpenters are going to get?"

Sarah couldn't believe what she was hearing. She hadn't signed on to be matron of the Children's Home in order to raise a raffle prize. "Because it's a baby! It's a human being! You can't make a raffle prize out of a person!"

"There you go, getting all emotional, Miss Carson. This is a business proposition no different than raffling that cow, horse, or house."

"I see it as very different, Mr. Coyne."

"Perhaps that is the reason I'm the director here and you are the matron. I'm a visionary. And you, Miss Carson, forget your place."

After Coyne's condescending words of caution, Sarah would have liked to walk out on him, but she needed this job and, in her heart, she truly believed the children needed her, too. They had little enough love coming their way and, she knew, most of what they did get came from her. These children were growing up without any advantages, and if she could soften things for them, just a little bit, for just a little while, that's what she was going to do.

As though reading her mind, the director said, "I suggest we pick one of the younger, newer babies. One you haven't had much time to get attached to. It's dangerous, you know, getting too attached to them."

How would you know that, Sarah thought. You avoid going into the wards. And when you do, you never smile or say a kind word to any of the children. They are merely charges. Responsibilities, nothing more, nothing less, she continued to herself.

Sarah couldn't live that way, despite Mr. Coyne's admonitions. Perhaps it was because she knew what it was like to sleep on one of those little cots in the ward. Sarah herself had been left at the Children's Home when she was only four, or about four; she couldn't be sure because she didn't know her actual birthday or age. She had only two memories of her life before the Home, memories that remained vivid because they visited her nearly every night. In the first, Sarah saw her younger self, kneeling on a low wooden stool over a big aluminum tub and washboard and scrubbing, scrubbing, scrubbing. The second memory was of a huge woman grabbing her by the back of her collar and throwing her down on the floor as easily as if she were a rag doll, sitting on her upper legs, then beating her with a switch for some unknown infraction.

She didn't remember how she came to be at the Home. All she knew was that one night she went to bed in that awful house and the next morning she awoke in a cot at the Home, where she lived for the next twelve years. When it came time to leave, Sarah couldn't see many choices for a young woman of her circumstances. So she stayed at the Home, trained as a nurse, and, ultimately, became matron to the continuous stream of children who came and went.

"Miss Carson, are you with me here?"

"Sorry, Mr. Coyne. You were saying?"

He sighed. "Yes, I was saying. We need to pick one of the babies for the raffle. A boy, I think. Everyone wants a boy. The healthiest one we've got. Any little one come to mind, Miss Carson?"

"No, Mr. Coyne."

"Then let me help you. Simply put, we will be doing this with or without your cooperation. Perhaps with or without you in our employ. So either you pick a baby, make sure it's a boy, or I'll go row after row, crib after crib, and find one myself. And you, Miss Carson, will find yourself looking for another job."

"How long do I have to make the choice?"

"Two days."

"What? I can't possibly ..."

Mr. Coyne cut her off. "Miss Carson, you have two days in which to choose the lucky tyke."

Lucky tyke, indeed, Sarah thought.

"Do we understand each other, Miss Carson?"

It took all she had to say, "We do, Mr. Coyne. Is there anything else?"

"No, Matron. Nothing else."

Sarah turned on her heel and began to walk out of the director's office.

"Oh, yes, and make sure he doesn't have lice!" he shouted.

As soon as she closed the door, perhaps a bit too hard, not quite a slam, but a bit harder than necessary, Sarah leaned up against the wall and let out a long, sad sigh. The children. The poor children. They were unwanted, deserted, suffering from the loss of one or both parents; and now they were to be commodities of exchange. It was so very wrong.

Sarah couldn't go into the ward just yet. She had to think. She knew when she was beaten, but she would be damned if one of her charges was going to be treated like a cow, a horse, or a house. She would be with the baby from start to finish, and on this she would not relent.

Sadly, Sarah knew it was Ernest she would pick. He'd only been with them a few weeks, but already she saw he had the bright, happy personality the director was looking for.

Little Ernie was healthy enough for the challenge. In fact, young as he was, he already had the look of someone who would thrive on challenge. And he didn't have lice.

Sarah didn't yet have a plan, but one thing was certain: She would not simply leave Ernie's fate to the whim of a random raffle ticket.

Tommy was more than a little smug about how slyly he'd dropped off Ernest on the stoop at the Home and kept an eye on him over the last few weeks. What he didn't know, however, was that Sarah had spotted him sneaking away when she bent down to pick up the basket, and its precious contents. She also saw him in the days after, as he watched the attendants stroll outside with Ernie and the other babies.

Tommy felt someone pinch his arm. Hard. "Ouch!"

Ignoring the yelp, Sarah whispered, "You. Follow me. Now." She led Tommy around the corner, out of sight of the orphanage and Mr. Coyne's open window.

Other than, "I'm Sarah," and "Tommy" in reply, no introductions were necessary. They'd seen each other often enough.

Tommy sure thought he was in for it, though. Boy, did he ever.

But when Sarah stopped walking, she turned sharply

around to face Tommy and, wasting no time, told him about the raffle. Her face was stony and her eyes vacant when she said it was Baby Ernest, Ernie, who was to be the prize.

"What? I left him with you so he would be taken care of. So he would be safe. I trusted you people. How can you do that? To raffle a baby like it's a cord of wood? A side of ham? That's shit."

"You're right, Tommy, and you're not telling me anything I don't already know. But it doesn't change the fact that a baby is going to be raffled, and that baby is Ernie. I've tried all I know to talk the director out of his heartless idea. If I keep harping on it, I won't have a job, and then Ernie will get raffled anyway, and all the other children will suffer as well. My hands are tied."

"What if I find someone to adopt Ernie?"

"It wouldn't do any good. Ernie has been removed from the rolls of available children. And even if he hadn't been, it won't stop the raffle. The director will just make me pick another baby in Ernie's place. He's convinced the trustees it will be good publicity for the Home and the children. I don't know how they can let themselves believe him. It's not as if he really cares about the children. In fact, I'm not sure he even likes children. It's himself he cares most about. Everything he does is measured against how it will further his career and elevate his social standing. He's such a, well, I don't know what. There aren't civilized words to describe what he is."

Tommy said, "Let me try for you. *Prick* comes to mind."

Sarah said, "Yes, that sounds about right. I have an idea, though, but I'll need your help."

"Go on."

Tommy couldn't recall a time he'd not been going to the boardinghouse with his ma. He kept himself busy with chores, but the real reason he went there was for the piano. His ma said his ear for music came from his da. He wouldn't know. He didn't remember his da. Tommy couldn't read music, either, but after hearing a piece once or twice he could play it back. He didn't know how he was able to do that, just as he didn't know why everyone else couldn't do it. Marta often told him how glad she was that she'd bought the piano from Mrs. Halverson. And playing it made Tommy a popular presence at the house, especially on quiet Sunday evenings after dinner. He was most glad for being able to play when he saw the look on Miss Eldri's face when she walked in and heard him playing "Song for Norway."

Tommy had found Eldri to be a nice addition to life at Marta's. She was surely different from her sister, not only in appearance but also in character. Marta was clearly the elder sister, the one in charge, while Eldri was the deferential younger one, but not too deferential. When necessary, Tommy had seen Eldri stand up to her full height, although still not nearly as tall as Marta, and hold her own.

Tommy hoped he was right about Eldri, because he needed her help. But first, he would talk to the elder sister.

Marta rolled over in bed and kissed John's shoulder. He smelled slightly of the cigar he'd smoked last night, the one she'd enjoyed sharing with him. Both the smell and the memory were quite pleasant.

"John?"

"Mmm?"

"I've something to talk to you about. It's important."

"You want another boardinghouse?"

She slapped him lightly on the shoulder she'd just kissed and pretended to pout.

John laughed. "You do many things well, Marta, but pouting isn't one of them."

"This is serious, John."

"Tell me. You're not…"

"No, no. I'm not. It's about Eldri."

"She's not?"

"No, not in so many words."

"Marta, I'm a simple man. We've only just started this conversation, and you've already lost me."

"Tommy came to me a few days ago. There's to be a raffle at the A-Y-P."

"Yes, I know, on Exhibitors' Day. It's late in the expo, September 18th, I believe. But what does it have to do with Eldri?"

"The Children's Home Society is going to participate. They're going to raffle a baby."

"They what? A baby? They wouldn't dare ..."

"They would. You know the girl who lives at Mary's? She's been helping Eldri lately."

"I do. Grace, right? I like her."

"Yes, Grace. I like her, too. We all do. She's the mother of the baby who is going to be raffled. The father was that Jack Barrett who was found dead a few months ago."

"No great loss. But, why would someone like Grace have anything to do with the likes of Jack Barrett?"

"He didn't give her a choice."

"Rape? Damn him, anyway."

"I think God did just that. Anyway, Grace is much better now, but the birth nearly killed her. She was in pretty bad shape, which is why Tommy took the baby to the Home the morning after he was born. He didn't know the matron saw him, or that she knew he was keeping an eye on the baby afterward. She's the one who told Tommy about the raffle."

"Does Grace know about this?"

"Not yet."

"What does this have to do with Eldri?"

"We need to be sure Eldri wins that baby."

"And just how do you intend to do that?"

"Well, we need to rig the raffle, of course!"

"Oh, of course. Why didn't I think of that?" John slapped his forehead with an open palm and eyed Marta skeptically. "I assume the winner has to be married to keep the baby?"

Marta nodded.

"Marta, think about this. Carefully. You intend to trick your sister into adopting a baby. This is the same sister who came to live with you because she had been tricked into getting married. Now you want her to embrace that marriage so she can take this baby? There's a certain irony here, but it's not amusing, and it's not right. You need to have more faith in Eldri. I've not known her long, but I'm confident I know her well enough to understand something of her character. Think how you would feel if the tables were turned. What if Eldri didn't believe in you enough to make the right choice? What if she felt she had to trick you into it?"

"What if she doesn't agree? Who knows where the baby will go?"

"Then we'll figure something out, although we both know it won't come to that. Eldri will agree. But Tommy needs to talk to her himself. After all, it's Eldri's life we're talking about. Not mine, yours, Tommy's, or anyone else's except that innocent baby and Ole Larsen. God help him. He's sure in for a surprise."

"I'd like to argue with you, John, but I can't because you're right. Could we pretend we argued, though? The making up is always so pleasant," Marta said with a mischievous grin on her face.

"You're incorrigible, and that is only one of the things I love about you. Come over here," said John.

CHAPTER 22

4th of July, 1909

Dear Eldri,

Happy Independence Day. Not for Norway this time, but for our new homeland, America.

The church hosted a big picnic to celebrate. It made me think about our picnic together. It seems so long ago now. Perhaps you think I bid on your basket only because I wanted the food inside. If so, you are wrong. I had to win your basket for the chance it would give me to get to know you better, without a bunch of people nosing around us.

Don't misunderstand me, the food was delicious. But the afternoon spent talking to you is what I will always remember.

If the sun hadn't gone down, and if folks didn't gossip so much, I think maybe we could have sat

under that lilac tree and talked through the
night. It seemed like you felt the same way.

I tell you again, that was surely my best day.

Your loving husband,

Ole

Eldri dressed that morning in her best white linen, draped
the red, white, and blue sash over her right shoulder, and
pinned it to the left side of her waist with a star-shaped
metal badge bearing the crest of the United States. She
pulled her hair back into its usual bun, tucked the stubborn
lock of stray hair behind her ear, and put on her straw
boater. In honor of the day, she'd removed the black
grosgrain ribbon from her hat and replaced it with a red,
white, and blue one. She laced and tied her black boots,
smoothed out her skirt, and walked down to the kitchen for
a fresh cup of Mary's morning coffee before leaving for
Ballard's Fourth of July parade. Having celebrated her
memories of Norway back in May, Eldri felt it only right to
celebrate the promises that had been fulfilled in America.

Marta was already in the kitchen talking to Mary about
meals and supplies. "Well, there she is. Elle, all you need is
a torch in your right hand, and you would look like Miss

Liberty herself!" Marta exclaimed.

Picking up her empty cup and pretending it was the torch, Eldri raised it high above her head with her right arm, slowly twirled around, and bowed at the waist before setting it down into its saucer so Mary could fill it with the dark, steaming coffee.

When the three women finished laughing over Eldri's spontaneous display of patriotism, Marta said, "You look so lovely. And it's wonderful that you're marching again today. You do realize what it says about you?"

"I'm not sure I do."

"Well, in my opinion, marching in both parades means you've learned to keep the best of Norway and yet embrace America now, too. And working so hard to learn English has been a big part of that."

"I had not thought about it that way, but, yes, I suppose you are right. This is my home now. While I will never forget where I came from, I do not feel like I'm a Norwegian living in America anymore. I'm just an American."

"Exactly my point, Elle."

"You have felt that way for quite some time, have you not? It has taken me a little longer."

"Yes, but I think now you understand when I said so long ago that America is where I belong. Now, out you go. Do us both proud, little sister. Hold your head high and wave the American flag for all to see."

"If it is all the same to you, Marta, I think I will just try to blend in. I am not the sister who likes to be noticed. But you are welcome to march with me and stand out all you want."

"Oh, no, no, no. I'll leave the marching and the parades to you, Elle."

"I will be on my way, then." Eldri winked and walked out the door to join the crowd gathering on Ballard Avenue.

The fourth of July. Sure didn't feel much like a holiday to Tommy. Felt more like the weight of the world was on his shoulders—or, at least, the weight of Ernie's world. He'd been certain Miss Marta would talk to Eldri for him and was more than a little rattled when she refused. But, she had also assured him that she was confident the conversation would go the way Tommy needed it to. He could only hope she was right.

Summoning his courage and mentally rehearsing what to say, Tommy went looking for Eldri. She wasn't hard to find. After marching in the parade earlier in the day, Eldri was back to doing the mending in her usual spot, next to the oversized window in the parlor, the afternoon sun shining in.

"Hi, Miss Eldri. Can I talk to you?"

"Ya, of course, Tommy. Oh, oh, you look serious. Something wrong with your ma?"

"No, no. She's fine, thanks. This is about Grace. And it is serious."

"Oh?"

"I need to tell you a secret, a big one."

"I can keep a secret, Tommy."

"I know you can, Miss Eldri. So here goes. Grace found herself in the family way. Fella named Jack Barrett took her last year and knocked her up."

"Knocked her up?" asked Eldri.

"Oh, sorry. Slang. The fact is, Jack raped Grace, and he got her pregnant."

"My God, how awful for her ..." Eldri softly set the piece she'd been working on into her lap and looked straight at Tommy. He had her full attention.

"Yeah, it was. She had the baby a couple months ago. A boy. Cute as he can be. The birth nearly killed her, though. Anyway, like I said, the baby was cute, except for also looking just like his pa."

"And where is the father now? In jail, I hope."

"Better than jail, Miss Eldri. He's dead, and I do believe it was not heaven where he went."

"How very sad."

"Count yourself lucky you never met him. He doesn't

deserve your pity or your sympathy."

Tommy continued with his story, being careful to protect Doc by leaving out his complicity. "Ma and I felt like Grace was too young and too weak to care for the baby. And it wasn't right that she had to live for the rest of her life not only with what Jack did to her in the first place but then with what came from it. So I put the baby into one of Ma's baskets, we made sure he was bundled up warm, and took him to the Children's Home. I set the basket on the stoop, rang the bell, and hid around the corner until I saw him taken inside. I've spied on the Home ever since, to make sure they're doing right by little Ernie. That's his name, Ernie. Well, Ernest. I named him after Grace's pa, who died."

"Ernest. A good name. But something's changed?" asked Eldri.

"Sure has. Well, nothing's changed yet; but it's about to. Do you know they're planning to have a raffle day at the world's fair?"

"I do not know anything except it is to be one of many special days on the program."

"Yeah, special. Listen to this: Somehow the director of the Children's Home thinks participating in the raffles that day is a good idea."

"Don't tell me ..."

"Yup. You guessed it. They're going to raffle a baby. And

that baby is little Ernie," replied Tommy.

"God in Heaven, how could they do that? How could they think that is a good idea?"

"I don't know, Miss Eldri, but the fact is, it's gonna happen."

"Still, why are you telling me all of this?"

"Well, it's kinda complicated, but here goes. I've gotten to know the matron at the Home. Turns out, she saw me drop off Ernie on that first night; and she also knew I was checking up on him. She's as pissed ... sorry, Miss Eldri ... she's as upset as I am about little Ernie being raffled, like he was no more than a stupid bar of soap or a wheel of smelly cheese. Miss Sarah—that's the matron, Sarah Carson—she can't stop the raffle, so we're both trying to figure out how to rig it. She needs me to find someone to win the raffle. Someone who will be a good mother to little Ernie. And, well, I thought of you, Miss Eldri."

Nerves were getting the better of Tommy, and his words started spilling out faster and faster. "Wouldn't you like to be a mother? I think you would be a wonderful mother. And if you adopted Ernie, I know it would make Grace happy."

"Uff da, Tommy. Please slow down. My English classes are going well, but not that well."

"Sorry, Miss Eldri. I'm a little nervous."

"Ya, I know you are, Tommy. And this is important. But that is also why you must slow down. I need to understand everything you are trying to tell me. Perhaps we could use some help. Do you mind if we ask Marta to join us?"

"I would really appreciate that," said a relieved Tommy.

While Tommy went to find Marta, Eldri used the quiet to collect her thoughts. But the fact was, although she might need Marta's help to fully understand what Tommy was saying, she didn't need Marta's help to understand what Tommy was asking of her. And she already knew what her answer would be.

When the discussion resumed and Eldri told her sister what Tommy had come to her with, Marta never let on that she already knew the story. Instead, she was carefully thinking through what she should say, because it would be important. Finally, "I know your heart, Eldri. And much as you try to be content here, you long for a family of your own. It's a family that will make your life complete. But there is a catch. The baby must go to a married couple."

"Married? I must be married? I suppose I should have thought of that, but I did not. So, Tommy, your idea won't work, because I am not married. Well, not really."

"In fact, Eldri, as far as Washington is concerned, you are indeed married. And if you agree to take this baby, your husband will have to be with you," said Marta.

"That means ..."

"Yes, you will have to decide to be with Ole," Marta said. "In order for Tommy's plan to succeed, you must bring Ole into it. It's important to that little baby. But it's important for you, too. As much as I love having you here, dear Elle, I know you aren't happy. This is just the place where you're waiting to find out what you're meant to do next. It's clear you miss your life in Conway. And I believe you miss Ole, too."

"What about his trick? Everyone knows how he made me look like a fool."

"Listen to yourself, Elle. No one but you thinks you a fool. It will be foolish, however, to let pride stand in the way of your happiness. Don't misunderstand me. Pride can be a good thing. But humility can be equally good. The tricky part is to know when to stand up for yourself and when you're only hurting yourself if you do. You need to decide which it is for you. But let's get back to right now, little sister. What are you going to do?"

"I must help that poor baby."

"Yes, you must and you will. That's who you are."

"You think too highly of me, Marta. The truth is, I'm just trying to figure out where I fit in this world and what I'm supposed to do with this life I've been given. Perhaps you are right. And perhaps I am meant to be in Conway with Ole … and Ernie."

"I believe you are." Marta smiled.

Tommy finally let out the breath he didn't know he'd been holding.

"Tommy, will you go get Grace?" asked Eldri. "The clothes in this pile aren't going to mend themselves, and I could use her help."

"Will you tell her about Ernie?" asked Tommy.

"She doesn't know?"

"No, Miss Eldri. I've not had the heart to tell her about the raffle."

"She must be told, Tommy. Maybe it will go better if we tell her together. What do you think?"

"I would sure appreciate that. If there's nothing else we need to talk about, I'll go get her."

"There's nothing else, Tommy." Eldri smiled at Tommy and Marta, put on her glasses, went back to mending the most recent split seam in one of Cissy's dresses, and was soon lost in her own thoughts.

Leaving Eldri alone in the parlor, Marta walked through the dining room and nearly knocked Mary over when she pushed open the kitchen door.

"Oof!" Mary gasped as she tried to regain her balance before Marta could tell she'd been listening against the door.

"I'm sure I needn't ask if you heard any of the conversation," said Marta.

"Any point denyin' it?"

"None."

"Then I'll just stick to sayin' thank you, Marta."

"It's not me you should thank. It's Eldri. Changing the

subject, what have you in mind to feed us tonight?"

"I've got a couple of hens roastin' in the oven. There are potatoes to boil and mash, carrots to peel and season. Fresh bread is comin' along, too. Should be enough leftovers for chicken and dumplins tomorrow."

"Sounds, and smells, heavenly. By the way, I'm sure you're bursting to tell Grace what you just heard; but if you do, you could very well ruin the whole thing."

"I swear, it's gonna kill me not to say anythin'. But I am tryin' to learn how to keep my mouth shut when I have to. It's not easy, though, I can tell ya!"

"I understand, Mary, but it's pretty important this time."

"I know, I know."

The first thing Grace did when she got to Marta's was sit down to a cup of tea with Mary.

"You alright, Mary? You're not saying much."

"I'm fine, lass. Just got things on my mind, is all."

"What things?"

"Just things. You know, this and that." Mary bit her tongue until she thought it might bleed. Mercifully, Grace let the conversation drop and soon went into the front room to help Eldri with her mending.

"Tea, Eldri? It's fresh," offered Grace.

"Ah, Grace. Yes, thank you. Here, would you please sew thus button back on Harald's shirt?"

"Of course."

"How do you think Cissy managed this one?" Eldri held up the dress she was working on. The bodice and skirt were nearly separated from each other.

"Were I to guess, I'd say it's because you didn't make the dress in the first place. We're never repairing your work, Eldri."

Eldri changed the subject, "Are you feeling well these days, Grace?"

"Why do you ask?"

"I've just learned what you've been through and how close you came to not being here with me. I am so very sorry."

Grace's lower lip trembled and her hands started shaking so hard she had to put down the shirt she'd been working on. "God, how does everyone know what happened to me?"

"Everyone doesn't know, Grace. Only a very few."

"It's just so shameful. I worry all the time about people finding out and what they will think of me."

"You? From what I hear, you did nothing wrong. And you have nothing to be ashamed of."

"Thank you, Eldri, but I will always wonder what I did to deserve what happened or how I could have prevented it. I trusted Jack. I was so stupid."

Eldri covered Grace's hands with her own. "This could have happened to any of us. Listen to me when I say, you have no blame in what happened. You didn't cause it, but you will survive it. No, what happened is between the man who harmed you and his maker. I am sure he's been trying to explain it ever since he got up there. I am also sure it hasn't gone well for him."

Grace hid half a smile.

"Would you bring Tommy in here, please?"

When the two young people came back into the parlor, Eldri looked up from her sewing. "Tommy, please tell Grace about Ernest."

"Ernest?" asked Grace. "My da?"

"Not your da, Grace, your baby." Tommy told Grace about the note he'd written when he'd taken Ernie to the Children's Home.

"Oh, Tommy."

"It just seemed right, Grace. Anyway, there's more, much more. You should sit down for this."

Tommy and Eldri spent the next hour telling Grace about the upcoming raffle at the A-Y-P and Ernie's impending participation in it.

"Oh, dear God. No." Grace sank so deeply into her chair it seemed she might disappear.

Tommy grabbed her shoulders. "Don't worry, Grace. We're working on a plan. And it's a good one."

CHAPTER 23

Eldri took over the conversation, explained Tommy's plan, and ended by telling Grace she was committed to becoming Ernie's new mother. She then told Grace about being married and how she'd come to be at Marta's house. "But Grace, I've learned Seattle is not my home. I want to go back to Conway. I want, I choose, to be Ole Larsen's wife ... and now, Ernie's mother. But you are Ernie's first mother, and I must know how you feel about this."

Grace took a moment to think, then trembled when she finally started to speak. "The idea of raffling Ernie, or any baby, is, well, just cruel. And, I didn't think it would be possible, but I feel even more guilty about Ernie now than I did already. Anyway, this is going to happen and I can't stop it, so, to answer your question, Miss Eldri, I cannot imagine a better mother than you. And if you say Mr. Larsen is a good man who will be a good father to Ernie, I believe you."

"I do, Grace, I truly do." And Eldri realized she believed it, too.

"But how can you make sure Eldri and Mr. Larsen will win Ernie?" Grace asked Tommy.

"We'll get that figured out. Don't you worry, Grace."

"I sure will worry until I see that Ernie is safe in the

care of Eldri and Mr. Larsen."

"Have I ever let you down, Grace?"

"No, never."

"And I'm not about to start now," Tommy said with firmly.

That evening after supper, Eldri excused herself and went up to her attic room. It was small, but not as small as the room she had shared with Anna in Conway and certainly not as small as the corner space and rude cot she and Marta had shared at the farmhouse in Norway. During the time Eldri had been living at Marta's, she'd added to the comfortable, but sparse, furnishings Marta had bought from Mrs. Halverson: a secondhand desk and chair, a good lamp for reading and sewing, and a few small photos, mostly of her and Marta. Her most recent addition, however, was also her most cherished. In a small, silver frame was the photo Alf had taken of Ole and Eldri, and Gus, on the day of that wonderful picnic. Ole had sent the photo to her as a Christmas gift. Eldri loved her little room. In her life, this was the first space she'd had all to herself. But she didn't love living in Seattle. She missed Conway and, yes, she missed Ole, too.

Before turning out the light of another day, Eldri sat down in front of the desk. Her composition was simple and

quite short, but it was the most important letter Eldri had
ever written.

July 4, 1909

Dear Ole,

*Happy 4th of July! Today, I marched in another
independence day parade. This time, it was in
honor of my adopted country.*

*Have you heard about the Alaska-Yukon-Pacific
Exposition? The A-Y-P? It's a huge world's fair
that is going on in Seattle. Perhaps you would
like to come down, and we could spend the day
there?*

*I have something to talk to you about. It is
urgent, and it is important.*

Affectionately,

Eldri

"Is she really inviting me to visit?" Ole tried to steady his
hands as he wondered what that one-sentence paragraph at

the end of her letter meant. Would she berate him for being such an oaf? Was she going to say that she never wanted to see him again? He probably deserved that. But there was no other way to find out what was on Eldri's mind than to accept her invitation.

Ole was not generally an impulsive person, the incident at the Mount Vernon courthouse being a huge exception, and here he was, about to act on impulse all over again. He decided to write Eldri straight away to accept her invitation, and he would deliver the letter in person. He hoped this second impulsive decision wouldn't backfire like the first one had.

Ole walked over to Alf and Anna's house. Until then, he had not told them that he had been writing to Eldri or that, since the new year, she'd been writing back. They were as willing to take care of things while Ole was away as he knew they would be. But when it came time to bring Gus into the house, Anna pinched her nose. "Must we?"

"It's only for a few days, Anna, and I've been very careful lately what I've fed her. So you and Alf won't suffer—well, not much anyway—from her rumblings internal."

"Oh, thank you. I feel much better," was all Anna said. But then she crossed her arms above her growing belly and gave Ole a wink.

Later that morning, Alf and Ole walked silently to the station, but as the train pulled into Conway, Alf said, "Good luck. I hope when you come home, it will be with Eldri."

"Thanks, Alf. Me, too." Ole grabbed his travel bag and stepped onto the train. He hoped he was doing the right thing. Boy, did he ever. He was gambling big on Eldri giving him a second chance, but if he mucked things up again, he didn't figure he'd get a third.

The train ride was long, loud, and uncomfortable. But it would get Ole to Seattle in just one day instead of the three it would take him in the wagon. So, he bided his time and dozed when he could. He was grateful for the generous lunch of cold chicken, fresh bread, and strong coffee Anna had fixed for him.

It was nearly dark when the train finally arrived at the Ballard Station. Ole was confused, and a little concerned, when he asked directions to Holm House because no one seemed to know what he was talking about. Finally, one old man—he was a hundred if he was a day—took his pipe out of his mouth, blew the stink of its smoke and his rotten teeth into Ole's face, and said, "Ah, you mean Halverson's. No one calls it Holm House. Too new." After getting directions, Ole gave the man a quarter, which he hoped would go toward the purchase of some tooth powder but guessed would probably go toward a shot of whiskey instead. Then again, he figured a whiskey would at least be something of a disinfectant for the inflammation in the old man's mouth.

When Ole arrived at the boardinghouse, "Holm House,"
it was Marta who opened the door.

"Yes?" she asked.

"Hello, is this where Eldri Lar... uh, Holm is living?"
asked Ole, removing the felt bowler Alf and Anna had given
him at Christmas.

"Who wants to know?"

"Her husband, Ole Larsen."

"What are you doing here?" an incredulous Marta asked.

"I have been writing Eldri ever since she left me. She
has recently been writing me back. She invited me to visit
her in Seattle. I decided to write and accept her offer, and
deliver the letter myself," Ole answered.

"Pretty bold of you, Mr. Larsen." Marta crossed her arms
defiantly. "And do you have any idea how Eldri will react to
hand delivery of this letter of yours?"

"I do not. But I would surely like to find out," Ole said
with equal defiance.

"I'll bet you would. I assume you haven't eaten." Ole
shook his head. "Well then, go through the parlor and into
the kitchen. Mary will fix you a plate. I suggest you wait in
there while I tell Eldri you're here."

"And you are?" asked Ole.

"I am Marta."

Ole's tone softened. "Ah, Eldri's sister. Thank you,
Marta."

"You're welcome. Maybe. I'll be back shortly, with or without Eldri." Marta headed up the stairs, several potential dialogs running through her head.

After rapping lightly on the door, Marta let herself into Eldri's room. "A minute?"

"Of course, Marta. What is it?"

"You have a visitor, downstairs, waiting for you."

"Me? A visitor? I don't have visitors. Do you know who it is?"

"I do, yes."

"And ... would you care to tell me who is this visitor?"

"No, I wouldn't. But I will anyway. It's your husband, Ole."

"Ole? Oh no, why? Why did he have to come—and why now? I only wrote him a few days ago. I need time. Send him away, Marta."

"I will not. He got your letter and has come all this way. Act like the grown up you are and go see him. It's time for you to get things figured out, and it's unkind to ignore him."

"And what he did to me? Was that not unkind? And now, he just shows up at your door?"

"Elle, it was not unkind. It was damned stupid, I'll admit. But I do not believe there was intentional unkindness. Now go downstairs and talk to the man."

"I don't suppose a crying fit or stomping around saying 'I won't, I won't, I won't' is going to work, is it?"

"No, it isn't. You know you need to fix this, not only for yourself, but also for Ernie."

"I hate that you're right."

"I know you do, Elle, but it doesn't change things. Now, stand up, straighten your skirt, and go. He's in the kitchen getting some dinner. Take off your glasses."

"The glasses stay on," said Eldri firmly as she slowly walked out from the security of her cozy room, down the stairs, through the entryway, parlor, and dining room, and, finally, into the kitchen.

"Hello, Ole."

Ole turned around to see Eldri for the first time in what seemed forever. How was it that she was the same but different, too? There was a certain composure and maturity that she'd not had before. Something else was different, but he couldn't see it.

"Oh, Eldri," was all he could say.

"The train ride from up North makes for a very long, rather uncomfortable day, I know. You must be tired."

"Eldri, your English. It's so …" Ole started. Then, "No, no, I'm fine. And your Mary here, she has just fed me much more than I should have eaten." He looked over at Mary, "Thank you very much for that fine dinner."

"Weren't nothin' more than I feed every strange man who comes down from the hills to court his wife," Mary said with a chuckle. "Best be on my way, though. Time for me to get home. Night, Eldri. Pleasure meetin' you, Ole. See you all in the mornin'," she said as she walked out the back door and into the summer night.

A minute later she was back. "Don't you go messin' up my kitchen while I'm gone."

"We will not, Mary. Good night," replied Eldri.

When Ole felt fairly certain he wouldn't be interrupted, he said, "Before I forget, Eldri, I got your letter and decided to deliver the answer myself."

"Yes, so I see. I suppose it is time we talked. We should go into the parlor. Would you like some coffee? Or perhaps something stronger?"

"Coffee would be nice, thank you."

While Eldri went into the kitchen to pour the coffee from the pot Mary always left on the stove, Marta came into the parlor where Ole sat waiting. "Well, you don't have any bruises, none I can see anyway, and you didn't get kicked out the front door. That's a start," Marta said.

Unable to think of an intelligent or clever response, Ole simply shrugged.

"Here's your coffee, Ole. Marta, you're here now, too? Coffee?"

Marta walked over to the sideboard in the dining room. "No, I think a brandy for me. Thanks. Either of you want to join me?" She looked over at the two. "Well, perhaps later. I'll be in my room if you need me," Marta said, looking toward Eldri, and started up the stairs.

For what seemed an eternity, both Eldri and Ole looked at their hands, their feet, the ceiling, out the window. Everywhere except at each other. Finally, Eldri stood up. "This silence is torture, Ole. You haven't come all this way just to deliver some silly letter and stare out the window."

"How do you want me to start, Eldri? With an apology? I can honestly say that I meant no harm. With anger? Why couldn't you have just given the idea of being married to me a chance before you decided you had to leave? With an offer? Come back to Conway, and I promise to make you happy. Or, perhaps, with the proposal you deserved in the first place."

"The proposal, Ole. You should have started with the proposal."

"Yes, I should have, Eldri, but I can't undo what's already done. I can, however, propose to you now. I think this is how they do it in America." Ole got on one knee, took out the one ring his mother had always worn, and said, "Eldri Holm, will you marry me? No, wait, too late for that. Eldri Holm, will you stay married to me?" Ole tried to give Eldri a charming grin. He hoped it worked.

"You need to apologize first."

"I just did."

"No, you offered to apologize. You didn't actually do it."

Ole moaned, then said again, "Dear Eldri, I meant no

harm, but I did wrong, anyway. Will you forgive me?"

"I forgive you, Ole Larsen," Eldri replied. "As for agreeing to stay married to you, I need to think about it."

"Seems like you've had plenty of time to do that since you left Conway. Are you just being stubborn? Please, Eldri, no games. I don't play them well."

"All right, then. Ole Larsen, I'll stay married to you, but on one condition."

"Condition?"

"That's right. There's a condition. We'll talk about it in the morning. We're both tired. Marta said you can sleep on the cot in the kitchen. Good night, Ole." And Eldri went up the stairs toward her room.

While Ole dragged his tired body to the cot by the woodstove in the kitchen, Eldri went up to Marta's room. Her door was already open.

"I assume you heard everything," Eldri said.

Marta shrugged. "Nearly so."

"Did I do the right thing? I mean, I was so mad at him before. How can I want to be with him now?"

"You love the man, Elle. But he hurt your pride. Remember our conversation about pride? You've been battling with yourself over that age-old question: What's more important? Happiness or pride? Some people choose pride. They're fools. You've chosen well. You've chosen happiness. Congratulations."

"That's all there's been to this? All the sleepless nights, the insecurity, the questions?"

"That's all, Elle. But, too, in the months you've been here you've gone from being a girl to a grown woman with a mind of her own. Ole sees that, too. But I think maybe he always knew the woman you would become, and that's why he wanted to marry you in the first place. He saw you as the woman he wanted to spend his life with. Embrace it, Elle. Some people are never loved as you are."

"Always the wise one, Marta."

"No, not always, Elle. But when it comes to love, yes, I know what it is to love and be loved. Now, go get some sleep. You have another hard conversation coming tomorrow."

"Ernie."

"Yes, Ernie. Good night, Elle."

CHAPTER 24

When Mary came into her kitchen the next morning, the last thing she expected to see was Ole asleep on the cot. Her cot, really, for those late nights at Marta's when she was too tired to make the walk home. It didn't happen very often, but when it did, Mary was thankful for that warm place to rest.

"Here you go." Mary handed Ole the first hot, strong cup of coffee of the morning. She figured he probably deserved it. "How was your night?"

"Truthfully, I'm not sure. But she didn't kick me out. Guess that's a good sign." Ole scratched the back of his head and tried to collect himself. "Thanks for the coffee."

"Well, first things first. Let's get some food goin'. Then you can work on figurin' out the rest of your life. Hopefully with Eldri and Ernie."

"Ernie?"

"Uh, oh. Did I say Ernie? Where did that come from?" Mary fumbled distractedly with the ties on her apron. "Sure, and I'd better get breakfast goin'," she said while rushing over to the cupboard to get the flour, salt, soda, and sugar to make the morning's biscuits.

"Well, that was certainly a strange conversation," Ole

muttered as he swung the kitchen door open and sat down at the dining room table. Eldri was already there.

"I see you were graced with the first cup of coffee this morning. That's Mary's little way of playing favorites, you know. Every morning, she picks who she's going to give that blessed first cup to. You're double lucky. Mary doesn't usually give it to a man. She must like you, Ole."

"Hopefully she sees something redeeming about me, Eldri. Hopefully, you do, too." He paused, but only for a moment. "Who's Ernie?"

"Where did you hear that name? Never mind, I know. The coffee queen in the kitchen. Ah, Mary. All right, Ole. I will tell you about Ernie."

Eldri wished she were confident enough to have this conversation in English, but she couldn't afford to make any mistakes, so she continued in Norwegian.

"Mary has a boarder at her house, a girl in her teens, who recently ran into some trouble. Wait, that is not right. Ole, I am not usually so blunt about such things, but what I am about to say is more important than trying to say it delicately. The girl who lives with Mary is named Grace. About a year ago, she was raped, and it left her pregnant. She has no family, so Mary took her in. Grace nearly died giving birth to a baby boy. And she would have, if not for Mary and her son, Tommy."

"Let me guess, Ernie," said Ole.

"Yes, Ernie. Well, Ernest, really. Grace is too young and was too weak to care for the baby, so Mary's son, Tommy, took him to the Children's Home Society, the orphanage. And the Home is going to raffle a baby at the A-Y-P. That baby is Ernie."

"My God," was all an incredulous Ole could think to say.

"Yes, that is how we all feel. Anyway, there are lots of folks who care about Grace and want to give her a chance for a happy life. And they want to do right by her baby, too. Neither Grace nor her baby brought any of this on themselves.

"Most of the folks who care about Grace and her baby are right here in Marta's house. They have asked me to agree to win Baby Ernie in the raffle. But in order to keep him, I must be married. There is a plan to, uhm, 'rig?' the raffle. Is that right word? Ya, that's the word Tommy used."

"So there you are, Ole Larsen. What this means is that I will stay married to you, and happily, I might add. And I look forward to going home to Conway. It is where I belong. I am hoping, though, that you will also agree to become Ernie's father and take both of us home."

Eldri watched Ole run his hands through his hair and scratch the back of his head and realized it was something he often did when he was thinking hard. Then he rubbed his chin, which needed a good shave. Eldri refused to let herself consider what Ole's hesitation might mean.

Finally, "You're saying yes, Eldri?"

"I am saying yes, Ole. If you still want to be married to me."

"Of course, I do. I came all this way hoping to hear you'll come home with me."

"And Ernie?"

"Ernie comes with us. Although, well, you do … uhm, you do want more children, don't you, Eldri?"

"Of course I do, Ole. It is like I told you during the picnic that day— I can think of nothing better than living the rest of my life with a good man in a home of my own that is filled with lots of noisy children. But Ernie deserves as much of a chance in life as any of us, maybe more."

"Then we will do our best to give it to him. I would be honored to be the father of Ernest Larsen."

"I hoped, I knew, you would do this."

"But Eldri, you don't know all the reasons I agree to it. True, I want to be with you for the rest of my life. Also true, that little baby deserves a fair chance. But more than that, perhaps I can give him the chance I never got."

Ole finally told Eldri about his life in Norway. "It was just Mor and me. We weren't around other folks very much. I never knew my father. In fact, I don't know for sure if my parents were actually married. My mother said so, but I think most folks in the village where I grew up didn't believe it. And when we came around, which wasn't often, they either scoffed at us, or just ignored us altogether. I tell you, though, being ignored was far better than hearing 'bastard' muttered aloud when we walked by.

"Mor wasn't a strong person, but she was my mother, and she raised me the best she could. We lived in a rented two-room cabin a safe distance from the judgmental heart of the village. You should know that there were some neighbors, a few, who, although they might not invite Mor and me in for a meal, they paid me generously for helping on their farms and Mor for her skilled piecework. I've never forgotten those small gestures of kindness.

"When smallpox ran through our village, it took Mor, and I knew that winter would be my last in Norway. Mor was only thirty-six when she died, but she had been tired of living for a long time. Without her, there was nothing to keep me in Norway. And I'd had enough of being scorned. I was sure that if I were to have any opportunities in life, America was where I would find them. My ticket to America was probably the easiest one the steamship agent in Kristiania ever sold.

"After the Atlantic crossing and months doing odd jobs all across America, I finally arrived in Conway, and I knew I was home. Good thing, too, because there wasn't any further west I could go, unless it was across the Pacific Ocean. And I was done with ocean travel. The crossing from Norway to America was plenty for my lifetime. I came through Seattle,

but I knew I wouldn't stay. Seattle was recovering from its
big fire and was well on its way to becoming a real city. I
must say I did enjoy the few days I spent here, the different
sounds, smells, and people. So many different types of
people. Have you ever thought about how mostly everybody
in Norway looks the same, Eldri?"

"I have."

"It's a funny thing. Anyway, I soon realized I wasn't
suited for living in a city. There are just too many sounds,
smells, and people. So I kept going until I found Conway."

"Ole, I had no idea."

"No one has, Eldri. I've not told anyone my story, until
now. So you see, I know the life Ernie might well have if we
don't take him."

Eldri walked over and gave Ole the hug he'd been
waiting for all these months. He hoped it wasn't out of pity,
but, truth be told, he didn't much care if it was. He reached
his hands down to each side of Eldri's face and pulled her
lips up to his. Finally, that kiss. The one he'd missed when
he'd dropped her off at Mrs. Brotvik's after that fateful day
at the courthouse.

"You're wearing glasses," Ole said as he tucked the loose
lock of hair behind Eldri's ear.

"You just noticed? Yes, I am, Ole. I'm seeing you for the
first time, in more ways than one." Eldri laughed and
hugged him again. "That reminds me, did you say there was

a letter? One you came all the way down here to hand deliver?"

Ole then had to admit there was no letter. "Eldri, I tried and tried to write, but the words just weren't there this time. That's when I decided I had to come here in person. I had to see you."

"You are hopeless, Ole Larsen."

"I suppose I am. You're not angry?"

"No, Ole, I am not angry. I'm tired of being angry. And it has taken me a little while to figure how much I am loved."

"That's good, ya?"

"Ya, Ole, that is good," Eldri said as she hugged her husband once again. Ole could only smile. He didn't completely understand what was happening, but he didn't care. He was happy for the first time in a very long time. It seemed Eldri was, too. Nothing else mattered.

It was time to make a plan.

Eldri and Ole called Marta and Mary into the parlor, then sent Tommy to fetch Grace from Mary's house.

A breathless Tommy was back a few minutes, and he was alone.

"Where's Grace?" Mary asked.

"Gone, Ma. Grace is gone."

"What do you mean 'gone'?"

"Just like I said. When I got to the house, Grace was gone."

"Sit down, Tommy, and tell us what you know," said Marta.

"When I went inside, I called and called for Grace. But she didn't answer. So I went through the downstairs. No Grace. When I finally went into her bedroom, it was empty."

"Empty? What do you mean 'empty'?" asked Mary.

"Too many questions, Ma. Please be quiet, and let me finish.

"When I got to Grace's room, her bag was gone. So were the two pictures she's always had with her. You know, the one of her parents when they got married and the other one of Grace standing with her ma and da when she was a little girl? And then I saw a fountain pen lying open and dripping ink onto her desk."

"So, did you find a note?" asked Ole.

"Not at first. But when I looked in the trash can, I found this." Tommy held up a crumpled sheet of paper with Grace's writing on it.

"Well, tell us what it says, boy!" Mary said.

"Okay, okay. Wait, my reading isn't so good. Miss Marta, would you?"

"Of course, Tommy."

July 20, 1909

Dear Tommy,

As I write this letter, my heart is breaking. It has been breaking ever since my ma and da died.

You say it's not my fault what happened to me. Still, I live with the shame of it every day. And, even though I have tried not to, I can't help thinking people are staring and whispering when I pass them on the street.

I now know Ernie will be taken care of and loved in a way I am not able to love him. I'm ashamed of that, too.

God bless you and your ma for all you've done. Please try to forget me. It will be better for you ...

"The letter ends there," said Marta.

"What are we going to do? We have to find her!"

"Wait, Tommy, you—we—need to do what Grace would want. We need to take care of Ernie," said Eldri.

"I can't just do nothing," Tommy protested as he jumped

up from his chair and started pacing the room.

"That is not doing nothing, Tommy; it is honoring Grace," replied Eldri. "You need to stay focused and help us save Ernie."

"Tommy, I will talk to John about hiring someone to look for Grace," offered Marta.

"Will he do that?" asked Tommy.

"I know he will. This will be difficult for you, but, please, let's see what John can do to find Grace while we take care of Ernie," said Marta. "Agreed?"

"Okay, but only until Ernie is safe."

Despite his distraction over Grace's disappearance, Tommy was the one who thought up the strategy they would use to rig the raffle. He was pretty good at card tricks and offered to teach the matron, Sarah, how to slip the winning ticket to the announcer. Of course, it was critical to the plan for Sarah to be the person who would draw the winning ticket. That way, they would be working with only one ticket, not thousands. But that one ticket and its two parts—one half in Eldri and Ole's hands and the other half hidden in Sarah's sleeve—would be critical. It was a simple plan, but all knew there was no room for a mistake.

"Piano, card tricks. Tommy, you never cease to amaze," said Marta.

"Don't forget blood donations, too, Miss Marta," he said with a sad smile.

Deciding Sarah should draw the raffle ticket turned out to be immeasurably easier than teaching her how to do it. She had never even held a playing card in her hands. Learning how to keep the raffle ticket from slipping down and out of her sleeve took a lot of practice. Pulling it out again on command, and without dropping it on the floor, well, that was an even bigger challenge.

The conspirators were all too aware of what could go wrong, but there was one thing that went absolutely without a hitch. When Sarah asked Mr. Coyne if she might be the volunteer to draw the raffle ticket, he was only too happy to agree. "You see? I was right again. I am thrilled with your change of heart, Miss Carson, and to so enthusiastically embrace this idea. It will be wonderful publicity for the Home."

"And the baby?"

"Yes, yes, it will be good for the baby, too."

Sarah couldn't stand the man. He was a weasel if there ever was one. All the more reason to get Ernie out of there and for her to stay to protect the rest of the children. She was more determined than ever to perfect the sleight of hand that Tommy was so patiently trying to teach her. Tommy had done his part and found the right parents for Ernie. Sarah would get her part right, too.

"I need to go home, Eldri," Ole said reluctantly. "But I'll be back next month for Exhibitors' Day and the raffle."

"Promise?"

"Absolutely." After a final hug and kiss, Ole put on his felt bowler.

"Alf and Anna were right, you know. You certainly do look smart in that hat."

Ole winked at his wife and rakishly ran his fingers along the front rim. Next, he grabbed up the traveling bag that held everything he'd carried to Ballard. It felt much lighter than it had when he'd left Conway a few days ago. Ole's steps felt lighter, too, and he may even have whistled a tune as he headed for the train that would take him north.

Alf was waiting when Ole arrived at the station in Conway. "Well?"

"I'll tell you everything, but not until we get back to your place, because we both know Anna is going to want to hear the whole thing, too."

"You're right about that. Come on. Let's get going."

When they arrived at the farmhouse, an excited Anna was waiting at the door. "I want to hear everything!" Both Alf and Ole smiled but said nothing. "First, though, we eat."

Anna had a hearty dinner waiting for them, and everyone was hungry, so dinner passed without much conversation.

"Anna, once again you've outdone yourself. Thank you," Ole said when he'd finished his meal.

"Yes, yes, enough of that. What about Eldri?"

Ole told Alf and Anna about his trip to Seattle, but not everything. He carefully avoided any details about Marta's unique boardinghouse and, as promised, her relationship with John. He told them about Eldri going to school to learn English and the skilled mending work she was doing for the people living at Holm House. Finally, he told them that Eldri was planning to come back to Conway.

"Well then, why didn't she come with you today?" asked Anna.

"Now that I know she'll be coming home, there's no hurry, Anna. Eldri has some things she needs to take care of."

"Things? What things?"

"Just things, Anna. Besides, Alf and I need to finish the last bit of work on the house. Once Eldri is back, there won't be so much time for that. And if we're really going to be farmers, there's a lot of planting to do before fall."

"I suppose, Ole. But I've missed Eldri."

"I know, Anna. And she's missed you, too. You have to be patient only a little longer."

"Not something I'm very good at."

"How well I know," Alf mumbled.

The meal finished and the kitchen cleaned, the three friends went out to the front porch so Alf and Ole could have a rare, but relaxing, after-dinner smoke.

The men pulled out the rolling papers, shook the loose tobacco in, licked the edges, and cinched the tobacco pouch. "It's good to be home. Seattle is fast becoming a big city, and that's fine for some. But I need to be surrounded by trees, not streetlights. Hard to see the stars over the lights," Ole said as he lit his cigarette.

CHAPTER 25

Sarah woke very early. This was the day and, knowing she wasn't going to fall back to sleep, Sarah got up and busied herself getting little Ernie ready and making sure she had the all-important raffle ticket that Tommy had managed to secure for her. Before she knew it, the cab, the expense for which Dr. Coyne reluctantly approved, was at the Home, waiting to take them to the fair. Sarah bundled up an excited and squiggly Ernie and pulled him tightly to her chest. "A big day for you, little man. Time to get on with it."

When they arrived at the A-Y-P, Sarah took Ernie directly to the Incubator Café, where arrangements had been made for him to wait until after the raffle. The director had thought it a stroke of promotional genius: a loving couple not only adopting a poor orphan but also one in an incubator. Sarah knew it would have been futile to point out that perhaps the loving couple would be none too eager to claim a baby sick enough to need incubation.

Finally, it was time. The raffle ticket, on which everything hinged, was tucked inside Sarah's cuff. It scratched her wrist and felt heavy as lead. As she walked up the steps of the Grandstand and over to the ticket barrel, she heard Tommy's advice going around and around in her head. "You need to be confident. That's the most important part of any card trick. And stay calm. If your hand shakes, you risk dropping the ticket and then the whole plan will fall apart."

Eldri and Ole arrived at the A-Y-P shortly after Sarah and Ernie. On their way to the Grandstand and the raffle, Eldri took Ole past the Incubator Café and told him about seeing the babies there when she and Marta visited the fair on opening day.

"Ole, I understand an incubator can be of help to a baby in distress. But look at these little ones. None of them seem distressed, at least not physically. They don't lack health. What they lack is parents. It is enough to break my heart, and I wish I could take all of them home with me."

"I'm sure you do, Eldri, but today we need to stay focused on rescuing just one orphan."

"You're right," Eldri said while taking his arm and letting him lead her away from the distressing scene.

Of course, neither Eldri nor Ole had any way to know that Director Coyne had made Ernie one of those incubator babies, if only for a few hours, and that, if all went as planned, they actually would be taking one of them home at the end of the day.

A rather bored-looking Master of Ceremonies quickly scanned his cue card and introduced Sarah. "Ladies and gentlemen, it's time for our next raffle. Miss Carson here is matron of the Children's Home. She has graciously offered to draw the ticket that will win one lucky couple a beautiful baby boy.

"Miss Carson, if you please."

Sarah nervously took the emcee's extended hand and let herself be escorted over to the ticket barrel, all the while worrying how long he would linger. If he stood over her when she reached into the barrel, it could affect the rest of Ernie's life. But Sarah needn't have concerned herself, at least not with that detail, because just as soon as they reached the barrel, the emcee dropped Sarah's hand and walked back to where he would be most visible to the crowd.

Sarah rolled the chicken-wire barrel around and around, then unlatched its small wooden door and reached in. As she did so, she slid the ticket out from under the cuff of her shirtwaist sleeve and down into her hand. She pulled her hand out of the barrel and gave the retrieved ticket to Director Coyne. To Sarah's everlasting relief, the sleight of hand worked perfectly, and her part in the ruse was nearly over. "Bless you, Tommy Miller," she whispered under her breath.

"Here we have it, ladies and gentlemen," an enthusiastic Coyne shouted out. "Tickets ready? The numbers are ..."

Eldri and Ole were being jostled about by the huge crowd, and just when Eldri tried to pull her half of the raffle ticket from her bag, a stranger bumped her arm. Eldri watch helplessly when, as if in slow motion, the ticket slipped from her hand and floated toward the ground.

"Oh, my God. The ticket! Ole, I've dropped the ticket!"

Ole managed to grab it up before it was swept away or mangled by the crowd of shoes surrounding it. He pressed the rescued ticket into Eldri's shaking hand and put a reassuring arm around her shoulders.

"0-5-1-8-1-9-2-9."

Ole looked at Eldri, and she nodded. "That's us! That's us!" Sarah looked out into the crowd. A wave of relief came over her when she saw the couple coming up to the grandstand to claim their prize. Eldri and Ole Larsen. Tommy had described them perfectly.

After comparing Eldri and Ole's ticket to the one in his hand, the unsuspecting Mr. Coyne announced, "Here they are, ladies and gentlemen, the happy couple who will be going home with a baby today. Congratulations!"

With one more raffle over, in a day full of them, the emcee stepped up and announced, "That's it for now, folks. Be back here in an hour, though, because if you thought the last raffle was exciting, at two o'clock we'll be raffling the Walnut Elephant from the California Building. You don't want to miss that one!"

Up on the grandstand, Sarah and Eldri tried to appear composed, but their tears of joy and relief gave them away. Mr. Coyne looked at Ole conspiratorially. "Women," he said, "they're just so emotional. Good thing they aren't allowed to vote."

Ole ignored the comment. He would not be drawn into the loathsome man's world.

Mr. Coyne allowed Sarah to escort Eldri and Ole over to the Incubator Building, where little Ernie was waiting. She rescued Ernie from his plastic box and brought him to his new parents, along with the forms required of Ole and Eldri before they could take Ernie home with them. Not that Eldri needed justification for her months of English study, but she was glad of them, nonetheless. This time, she could read every word on the forms she was signing.

"Oh Sarah, he's beautiful. And healthy. You've taken such good care of him. We promise we will, too."

"I know you will, Eldri. You, too, Ole. Indeed, he is beautiful and healthy," Sarah said. "And now, he has a chance to be happy."

The night should have been a celebration of unqualified joy at Holm House. John was able to get away from Charlotte by claiming he had to go on a short business trip. Wisely, Charlotte had put up no protest. Mary had spent the day cooking and had outdone herself. Sarah was there, too, Tommy having delivered her a personal invitation from Marta to join them for the evening. But Grace's absence cast a pall over the gathering.

Ole, Eldri, and Ernie spent the afternoon wandering through the A-Y-P and being photographed by reporters, especially those from the *Seattle Times* and the *Seattle Post-Intelligencer*. When the new family finally walked through the door, they couldn't believe the crowd waiting for them. Mary was rushing in and out of the kitchen, John stood with his arm around Marta's waist, and then there was Sarah sitting in a corner chair, smiling. Marta had also invited the residents in the house—Fred and Florence, Albert and Cissy, and Susannah—to join them. All in all, it was a rather large crowd to entrust with a secret as important as the circumstances of Ernie's adoption. But for this group, keeping secrets was a way of life. It would perhaps be most difficult for Mary, but there was too much at stake, and Mary knew this was one secret she would never let slip.

Eldri looked around the room at the group of people who had done such good for this one little boy, and it filled her heart.

Marta opened a bottle of champagne. John warmly shook Ole's hand and raised his glass to him, "Congratulations to the new father."

"Thank you," said Ole.

John then picked up a knife from the dining table and gently tapped it against his champagne flute. "A toast, to Eldri and Ole. May they enjoy a long and happy life together with their son, Ernest Larsen."

After the toast, John said, "Ole, will you help me, please?"

Everyone, even Marta, wondered what John was up to when he led Ole out the back of the house. But the mystery was soon solved when the two men came back into the room carrying a cradle elaborately painted with the most beautiful Norwegian Rosemaling any in the room had ever seen. "For Ernie," was all John had to say.

"John Harris, this time you have quite outdone yourself," Marta said as she took his arm again. "How did you manage it? And keep it a surprise?"

"Well, Marta, I know people who know people, and so it goes," John replied with a smile.

"Words fail, John. But know this cradle will be an heirloom we will cherish for Ernie." Eldri's voice cracked.

For reasons everyone understood, Tommy had been quiet throughout the evening; but eventually he could contain his question no longer. "Mr. Harris, Marta said you would hire someone to find Grace. Did you?"

"Yes, Tommy, I did. He's supposed to be the best private detective in Seattle. Unfortunately, there is no news yet. I must warn you, when Grace said how much she misses her parents, it might mean ..."

"I know what it might mean."

Harald was in Chicago, and Marta had his permission to put up visitors, at her discretion, of course, when he wasn't in residence. Sarah was offered a night away from the Home and gratefully accepted the invitation to stay in Harald's room.

John took Marta's hand as they went upstairs. Ole looked at Eldri, a question in his eyes. She answered by taking his hand and leading him toward her attic room. But first, she turned to Mary, who was holding Ernie and looking reluctant to let him go any time soon. Mary gave a wink and a nod, and Eldri continued up the stairs with her husband. Tommy had hoped he would be walking home that night with a happy Grace, but he went alone instead.

When all was finally quiet, Mary held up the little one she'd helped Grace give birth to. "You're lookin' a far cry better than the last time I saw you. And damn, oops, watch your mouth, Mary. I'll be darned if you don't look even more like your da than when you were born. That curly black hair, those blue eyes. I do believe they actually twinkle when you smile. And about that smile. It holds the same charm as your da's smile. But I can already see it don't hide a black heart like his did." Mary sat next to the stove in the kitchen for a long time and rocked the dozing baby, but she eventually put Ernie in his new cradle and settled into her cot next to him. When all else was quiet, Mary couldn't help hearing the other muffled rocking that had started in one of the rooms upstairs, and it made her smile. "Sure, and maybe you won't be an only child for long," she said.

CHAPTER 26

While she was packing up her things and getting ready to go home to Conway, Eldri dreaded the idea of going back to Mrs. Brotvik's, or whatever the boardinghouse was now called, or, God forbid, living at the logging camp. Ole just kept telling her not to worry about where they would live, but Eldri couldn't help it.

When she'd emptied out the last drawer in the oak dresser and Ole had taken her case downstairs, Eldri went looking for Marta.

"We don't have much time left together, and I wanted to share a few minutes with you before I go."

"Oh, Elle, I used to think you looked just like Mor. But now, you look just like, well, you."

"How much I've learned over this past year, Marta. And how much I'm going to miss you. So much it hurts."

"You won't be far away. And if I don't have to see that awful Mrs. Brotvik, God rest her soul, you can know I'll be visiting you, my brother-in-law, and my nephew. John has also talked about traveling together when he goes up north."

"Oh, I hope so, Marta. You're Ernie's only tante, you know, unless you count Dagmar as his other aunt, which I don't. And I now understand why you love John as you do."

"Thank you, Elle."

A long, last embrace and the sisters parted ways, once again, Marta to stay in Seattle, where she belonged, and Eldri back to Conway, where she at last knew was where she belonged.

Later that day, as the early autumn sun was setting, Marta poured two whiskeys and walked into the kitchen.

"Here we find ourselves, Mary."

"Indeed we do, Marta. Indeed we do. Cheers."

Eldri and Ole were quiet while they watched the city fade into the distance and the landscape transform into the wooded hills and lowland fields they were accustomed to in Norway. And then there they were, back in Conway. When he wasn't sleeping, Ernie had been a happy distraction from the tedium of the long train ride.

As the train pulled into the station, the new Larsen family saw Alf and Anna waiting on the platform. Eldri's eyes lit up at the sight of Anna, and, the first chance they got, Anna and Eldri rushed up to each other. They hugged, let go, looked at each other, then hugged again, oblivious to their husbands hauling the bags, and Ernie's beautiful cradle, into Ole's wagon.

Ole had not told Eldri about Anna's "condition." Nor had he told Anna that Eldri now had a baby of her own. He got something of a tongue lashing from both women over that, but it was a good-natured one. "How could you not tell us, Ole?" the women had said, nearly in unison.

"Well, maybe I'm finally beginning to figure women out because I knew I was going to be in trouble either way. Anna, if I told you about Ernie, then Eldri would be mad I hadn't let her tell you. And, Eldri, if I told you about Anna, then Anna would be mad at me. So I figured if I kept my mouth shut, and said nothing, you would both be mad, but not as mad as if I had spilled your beans. So that's what I chose to do."

"Well, when you say it like that, I guess you're right. We forgive you, Ole. Don't we, Anna?"

"Ya, ya, we do."

Anna was all over Ernie, and although she was finally comfortable with English, Eldri was happy listening to Anna speak in the lovely cadence of their native Norwegian. "Oh, Eldri, he's beautiful. Look, he's smiling at me!"

"I think it's only gas." Anna ignored her husband's remark, reluctantly gave Ernie back to Eldri, patted her own growing belly, and gave a big smile.

"I am so happy for you and Alf," Eldri said. "When is the baby due? How are you feeling?"

"The best I can figure, it'll be coming sometime in

December. Except for being tired enough to go to bed right after supper, I'm feeling very well. I was a little mad at you early on, though, because I was so sick, and I didn't have you to whine to. But I've forgiven you."

"Oh, Anna, I do wish I'd been here. But I had to go."

"I know, Eldri. But, you've changed in so many ways. You're such the city girl now. Are you sure you'll be able to stand the slow life here?

Eldri was being honest, with her friend and herself, when she answered, loudly enough to be sure Ole heard her, "Anna, now that I've had a chance to make the choices for my life for myself, I can't imagine living anywhere else, with anyone else." A satisfied grin came over Ole's face as he finished loading up the wagon.

There was so much to catch up on. Anna excitedly told Eldri about the beautiful house Alf had built for her, with lots of help from Ole. "It's out on the flats on Fir Island, just down the road from the river crossing. The sitting and dining rooms are in the front next to the stairs. Three bedrooms upstairs. And an attic for storage. The kitchen matters most to me, and Alf gave it special attention. But, of course, Alf wasn't being entirely selfless. He cares about eating my food as much as I care about cooking it ..."

"So I figured if I built Anna the kitchen she wanted, she would be happy, and I would never go hungry," Alf added.

Eldri smiled at the thought of Alf now finishing Anna's

sentences.

Once in the wagon and on their way, Eldri asked, "Ole, don't you think it's time to let me know where we're going to sleep tonight?"

"Soon, Eldri." Ole smiled.

"Anna, you're smirking," Eldri said. "What do you know?"

"Nothing, Eldri."

"I don't believe you."

"Ole, this is too hard," Anna pleaded.

"Anna, you promised," Ole chided.

"Uff."

The mystery deepened. Eldri watched as they passed the road that would take them to the logging camp. She was relieved. The boardinghouse wasn't much, but it was certainly better than the camp. And then, they passed the boardinghouse, too.

"The boardinghouse looks deserted, Ole."

"And so it is."

"Why?"

"I don't really know. I have heard rumors, though, that there was no will, which means the boardinghouse will go to Gudrun's next of kin."

"I think that might be Tante Lena."

"You might be right, Eldri. I guess we'll find out eventually. In the meantime, the condition of the boardinghouse just keeps getting worse."

"How sad."

"Yes."

"So we are not staying there?" asked Eldri.

"No one is staying there, for now," answered Ole.

That left Eldri really curious. Nothing to do, though, but wait because no one was giving anything up. So she hugged an exhausted Ernie and tried to be patient.

Ole led the horses and wagon onto the barge, and the group crossed from Conway to Fir Island. They passed the island church, then drove slowly past a tidy, new farmhouse. Anna said, "There's my new house, Eldri."

"So perhaps we will spend the night with Alf and Anna?" Eldri asked. Ole, Alf and Anna stayed silent while the wagon continued its slow movement.

Finally, a few yards farther down the road, they arrived at a second farmhouse, another tidy, new farmhouse, much like Alf and Anna's. Gus came running from around the backyard to greet them.

Next, Eldri noticed the small lilac tree planted next to the house and looked at her husband.

"It is a cutting from the tree we sat under at our picnic. Do you remember what you said about lilacs?"

"I do remember."

"Welcome home, Eldri."

EPILOGUE

Saturday, 8 September 1962

"Hurry, Gran! We need to go!" Grace called from the bottom of the stairs while she paced around the small Oriental rug, twirled a piece of her long, wavy hair, and checked her watch.

"Calm down, Grace, there's still plenty of time."

"Daddy, please. Elvis has been shooting his new movie all week, but this is his only Saturday there. And if we don't get there early, it will be so crowded I won't have any chance of getting his autograph. And, if I don't, I'll die for sure!

"You'll die?" her dad said with a wink.

"Come on, don't tease. You know what I mean."

Listening from the upstairs guestroom of her son's home, Eldri smiled while she adjusted her hat and tucked a lock of white hair behind her ear.

Ernie poked his head in. "You ready, Mom? I don't think Grace can stand to wait much longer."

Eldri stepped into her shoes and picked up her pocketbook. "Ready, son."

When Grace saw her grandmother coming down the stairs, she ran up to meet her and grabbed her arm, nearly knocking Eldri over. "Ooph, sorry, Gran. Come on, though, this is going to be such fun. You've never seen anything like it. Elvis is soooo dreamy! And then we can ride the Monorail, the Bubble-ater, and the Space Needle! If we're lucky, maybe I'll even win a bear for you at the Arcade!"

Eldri hugged her granddaughter, but turned to look at her son, "A bear? Well, that would surely be the second most special thing a lucky girl could win at a world's fair."

When she walked out of the house, Eldri gazed up at the bluebird sky, absent-mindedly ran her hand across the old brass plaque that, after all these years, was still above the doorbell, "Holm House," then joined Ole in the back seat of Ernie's car.

ACKNOWLEDGMENTS

Thank you to the many family members—especially my mother, sisters, and children—and friends, who patiently listened to me recount the novel's latest updates and provided constant encouragement.

Special thanks to Jennifer Lally, Christina Miles, Michelle Plants, Christine Pinto, Tori Peters, Michael Crowson, and Mike Markel for reading and reading my many drafts and for your invaluable edits, comments, and observations. Any errors or omissions, however, are mine alone.

NOTES

This book is a work of fiction, but some elements of it are based on real events.

The idea began with a story about my great-grandparents, Ole and Eldri Holm, who actually did go to the courthouse in Mount Vernon to witness the marriage of two friends. While there, Ole, practical Norwegian that he was, asked the judge to marry him to Eldri, and the judge complied. It wasn't until they got back to Conway, and Eldri tried to say goodnight, that Ole told her they were married. Eldri was "just so mad" and refused to speak to him. A few weeks later, there was a picnic-basket auction at the church they both attended. When Eldri's basket came up for auction, Ole knew he'd better win it, whatever the price. He did, and they shared a nice lunch. After the picnic, Eldri decided maybe Ole wasn't so bad after all, and she finally agreed to go home with him. They lived all their married life in a farmhouse on Fir Island, Washington. There was a lilac tree in the yard.

The story of an orphaned boy, Ernest, being raffled at the Alaska Yukon Pacific Exposition on Exhibitors' Day is also true. However, no one claimed Ernest, and his fate remains unknown. Displaying orphaned babies in incubators was popular at several early world's fairs, including Chicago's White City. Although promoted as premature and in need of incubation, the babies were more likely healthy and full-term.

In its four months, the Alaska Yukon Pacific Exposition hosted 3.7 million visitors. Admission was fifty cents.

On September 30, 1909, President Taft visited the A-Y-P in person.

In all, nearly eighty buildings occupied the site, and after the exposition closed, those buildings were given to the University of Washington; but just one year later, most of the buildings were gone. They were never intended to be permanent. However, the Cascade Fountain, now Drumheller Fountain, remains on the university's campus today.

For more information about the history of early Seattle, visit a local website: Historylink.org. And for more information about the 1909 Alaska-Yukon-Pacific Exposition, consult *Washington's First World's Fair, Alaska-Yukon-Pacific Exposition, A Timeline History* (History Ink/HistoryLink in association with the University of Washington Press, 2009), by Alan J. Stein, Paula Becker, and the Historylink staff.

An interesting read about the 1962 Seattle's World's Fair is Jim Lynch's novel, *Truth Like the Sun* (Bloomsbury Publishing, 2012).

Skagit Settlers: Trials and Triumphs, 1890-1920 (Skagit County Historical Society, 1975) proved to be an invaluable resource for learning about early twentieth-century life in Conway and Fir Island, Washington.